THE VERY WORST THING

TOREY HAYDEN

THE VERY WORST THING

■ HARPERCOLLINS*PUBLISHERS*

Library of Congress Cataloging-in-Publication Data

Hayden, Torey L.

The very worst thing / Torey Hayden. — 1st ed.

p.   cm.

Summary: David has never had a permanent home or a real friend,
but when he decides to try to hatch an owl egg with the help of a
classmate, his life slowly begins to change for the better.

ISBN 0-06-029792-1 — ISBN 0-06-029812-X (lib. bdg.)

[1. Foster home care—Fiction. 2. Friendship—Fiction.
3. Schools—Fiction. 4. Owls—Fiction.] I. Title.

PZ7.H313888Ve 2003   2002010586

[Fic]—dc21   CIP

AC

Typography by Amy Ryan

7 8 9 10

First Edition

For the loving memory of
Dandelion and Tigger Tom,
whose small deaths brought forth this book.

ONE

David kept a running list in his head called "The Very Worst Things." Number 22: Going to the dentist. Number 18: Going to the dentist and finding out you had two cavities. Although when it came time to get the cavities filled, it moved right up the list to about number eight.

David was always wondering what other people put at the top of their list, because he noticed what strange priorities some people had. They only thought about immediate things, like not getting to go someplace they really, really wanted. Or having to wear something stupid, so that people might laugh. Truth was, while these were bad things, they didn't last. It was the stuff you got stuck with forever that mattered. David knew that.

He also knew what the very worst thing was. It was nothing. When there wasn't anyone who cared what happened to you. When you didn't belong anywhere or to anyone. That was Number One on the Very Worst

Things list. David knew, because it had happened to him.

David didn't even remember his dad. He had left before David was old enough to talk, much less remember anything. All he knew was that his dad had curly hair, and David had only guessed that, because he and his sister Lily both had curly hair but their mother didn't. But that was it.

Truth was, David didn't remember his mother much better. All he had was a picture he'd made up from what Lily used to tell him: how his mother had long, kind of messy hair—"skinny hair," Lily had said, because it lay flat on her shoulders, and how she was kind of fat. Lily had said it was okay she was fat because this made her nice and squishy when you hugged her. David didn't know about this, because he couldn't remember hugging her or her hugging him. All he could remember was the shouting. Or maybe it wasn't shouting. Maybe it was just birds making noise, because once Lily had told him that there were crows living in the chimney. But David didn't think crows lived in chimneys. He'd always thought it was shouting.

The only thing David definitely did remember was the lady coming to take them away. She'd worn a brooch with a tiny, tiny rose stuck inside a clear plastic block that looked like a dinky ice cube, and he'd wanted to touch it. David remembered that rose brooch so well, but somehow he'd forgotten his mother.

Then the foster homes started. There'd been six of them, one for each year since he and Lily had been taken away. He hadn't always known why they'd kept moving from place to place, because people didn't think they had to tell kids reasons for stuff like that. Some of the time, though, he knew. Like with the Soames. They were going to adopt him and Lily and that's what they said when David and Lily first came. "We're going to be your real mom and dad from now on," they'd said, "so you can call us that, and this will be your new home." But in the end, no. They changed their minds.

"It's 'cause you're retarded," Lily had said to him. She was ten that year. "No one wants a six-year-old baby. You can't talk right. You can't learn anything at school. You can't do anything except wet the bed. It's your fault this is happening to us." David knew she was right, because he'd been standing just outside the door when he heard Mrs. Soames say to the social worker, "He's just such a lot of work."

Sometimes, though, it was Lily's fault, but she'd never admit it. She had a terrible mouth on her and she was always stealing stuff from other kids. And at the Andersons' she'd set fire to the kitchen curtains because she said she wanted to call a fire engine. That was the end of them living there. Then the year she turned eleven she started running away and she kept running away, whether anybody had done anything to her or not. The truth is, nobody's going to put up with a kid who won't stay in one place. So Lily wasn't as smart as she thought.

Lying on his bed, David stared at the wall. Lying on *someone else's* bed. Not his bed. He didn't even have a bed.

Not of his own. He knew he was experiencing the Very Worst Thing right now. And this time he didn't even have Lily. Mrs. Mellor had told him that the judge felt Lily would be better in a "home" this time, which was really just another way of saying a kids' jail, a place that had locks on the windows and the doors and even the refrigerators. So, for the first time, David had had to come to a new foster home alone.

Mrs. Mellor was his social worker. She had a big square body and always wore sludgy-colored suits—sludgy blue and sludgy gray and sludgy green—as if there were a special store that sold nothing but social-worker suits. Her head looked too small to David, like a rock waiting to roll off Sludge Mountain, but mostly he didn't look up there. When she talked, he watched the buttons on the jacket of her suit heave up and down. He didn't know why he watched them so carefully. They were just buttons. But he sort of had them memorized.

This time Mrs. Mellor came to tell him he was going to stay with "Granny." Geez, *Granny.* What kind of name was that? David pictured a character out of one of those children's books teachers read aloud after lunch: someone old and jolly who had ninety-two pictures of other children she had saved, plus a snotty little misfit at her heels you were going to learn to love having follow you around, and probably she was carrying a freshly baked apple pie in her hands.

As it turned out, Granny wasn't exactly like that. She *was* old; that was a good guess, although the name sort of gave it away. But she didn't seem especially jolly. If she'd had any other foster children, she didn't say, and he was the only kid there. In fact, he was the only other *person* there. There didn't even seem to be a Mr. Granny.

Granny was small. At eleven David was as tall as she was and he wasn't very tall for his age. She was skinny and dry looking and her hands had knobby, wrinkled knuckles. She hardly talked at all after Mrs. Mellor left. Instead, she took him up to his room.

His room was in the attic. To get there they had to go up a weird little staircase behind a door in the kitchen. Seeing the door, David had thought it was just a closet, but when Granny opened it, it was almost like a secret passage upward. This would have been cool if it had been better lit, but as it was, David felt a bit spooked. The steps were so small he could fit only the front part of his foot onto them and so steep he wanted to climb them using his hands, too. The stairwell had only a dim light at the very top and was so narrow that when he put his elbows out, David could touch both sides.

The stairs were tiny but the room at the top was huge. It had a dinky window at the far end almost level with the floor, so that he had to bend down to look out. The ceiling sloped steeply down on either side so that David could stand upright only in the center of the room. And there was an iron bed. David had never seen a real iron bed before. When Granny was gone, he bounced on it. It was like a trampoline. And it smelled. Not bad. Just old. Old and not used, like it was nobody's bed.

David waited until Granny had gone downstairs, and then he opened his suitcase. Little Blanket was in the corner of the suitcase beside his second pair of shoes. Lily used to tease him so bad about Little Blanket. She was always taking it and hiding it, because she said he was such an embarrassment to her when he acted like a baby. Once when she was in a rage, she tore it in half; so now it really *was* a little blanket.

Lying down on the bed, David pressed Little Blanket over his eyes. Lily was right, of course. He was way too old to have a baby blanket, even a handkerchief-sized one, but it was the only thing that had been with him forever. He kept it because it smelled familiar.

TWO

"Davison, you'll have to hurry up if you want breakfast," Granny hollered. The narrow little staircase pumped up her voice like a megaphone.

David's limbs felt like they'd been turned to stone. Heavy. Slow. He pictured himself as a coming-to-life statue, stumbling awkwardly toward the staircase.

"Your clothes aren't on straight," Granny said when she saw him. "Do you know how to button?" She didn't say it in a nasty way, but she reached over and pulled his shirt down as if he were a five-year-old.

David jerked away.

"Don't get snooty. Mrs. Mellor told me you have a hard time with some things. I understand."

"I-I can b-button. I'm not a b-baby."

"Well, then, button proper or we're going to be late," Granny replied. "I do for Mrs. Worthington this morning. Got to be there by nine-thirty."

She was a *cleaning* lady? *That* was her job? How did she

ever get foster kids? How had he ever ended up here? David looked around. It was a small house. Not poor or anything, but not really nice either. Probably she did it for the money. Took in kids like some folks took in ironing.

Mrs. Mellor had told him he wasn't going to ride a bus to school, like in the city, so when David stepped outside, he looked for the car. It wasn't in the garage. The garage doors were the old-fashioned kind that folded back, and one of them was broken, so there hadn't been a car in there for a long time. He looked at the cars out on the street. His dad had a Cadillac. At least that's what Lily said. Parked in front of Granny's was a Ford Escort. It was a vomit-beige color and about a million years old. Annoyed, David headed for it.

"It's not that far," Granny said. "We're going to walk."

Walk?

Everything here looked the same to David. The streets had just houses. No stores or gas stations or fast food places, like in the city. Was he going to have to walk a million miles to school every day? How come she didn't use her car like a normal person?

Before he knew it, they were there. School. Probably Number 2 on the Very Worst Things list.

In the school office, the principal smiled and shook David's hand in that way adults do when they want you to think they are treating you as if you were another adult. His name was Mr. Dawson. "David is going to be in Mrs. Hallowell's fifth-grade class," he said to Granny.

"*F-fifth* grade?" David cried. No one had said anything

8

about putting him into fifth grade. He was in *middle* school. He was in the *sixth* grade, not fifth! You couldn't get flunked in the middle of the year, could you? David tried to get the words out to explain all this but his tongue wouldn't work that fast.

Mrs. Hallowell met them at the classroom door. She had blond hair and a broad, friendly face with freckles on it. She wasn't very old for a teacher and David would have thought she was pretty, if he hadn't been so worried about this fifth grade/sixth grade mixup.

She showed him to a table where three other boys sat. Leaning over him, she set a sheet of math problems down. "Can you do adding?" she asked.

The boy directly across from him sniggered.

"There's a m-mistake," David said. "I-I'm supposed to be in the sixth g-grade. N-not in fifth."

"Well," Mrs. Hallowell said in a warm, relaxed voice, as if what she was saying were perfectly all right, "some of the schools in the city aren't quite up to where we are in this district. There's a lot of material you won't have covered."

"B-but I'm in *middle* school!" David said.

"Yeah," whispered the kid across from him. "And I'm in college."

David couldn't do the work. He couldn't do the math paper Mrs. Hallowell gave him. He couldn't read the social-studies book. He couldn't even manage the news magazine and that was mostly pictures. Everything looked all squabbled up on the page. Bracing his forehead with one hand, David stared at it.

Mrs. Hallowell had been walking around the class as everyone worked. She stopped at David's desk. "That's all right," she said when she saw all David's erasure marks. "Tomorrow you'll be going to see Mrs. Chisholm for reading and math. She helps our special learners."

David's shoulders sagged.

"Don't worry. It's hard to adjust to a new school. I understand."

David was thinking that at about Number 15 on the Very Worst Things list were teachers who thought they understood.

The next time Mrs. Hallowell came over, it was just before lunch. She said, "When someone new comes into the class, we always choose someone to be their 'shadow,' to help them find their way around. This is Rodney, and he's going to be your shadow. He'll show you where the lunchroom is."

It was the kid who sat across from David.

"I didn't want to do this, so don't get any idea that it means I'm your friend," Rodney said when Mrs. Hallowell was gone. He was shorter than David and had dark red hair in a floppy style that kids would have made fun of at David's school in the city. But not here. There was a little strut in his walk that showed he knew he was hot stuff. And he was cocky, even to the teacher.

They got in line in the cafeteria.

"You flunked, didn't you?" Rodney said.

David didn't answer.

"Man, you must be world-class stupid to get flunked in the middle of the school year." His voice had an amazed note.

David wished desperately that the line would move faster.

"Are you retarded?"

David didn't answer.

As the line inched forward, Rodney leaned over to the boy in front of them. "This kid's in the wrong class all right. He should be in that special class at Jefferson School."

The other boy thought this was really hilarious. Both of them hooted like startled baboons.

Trying to ignore them, David picked out a plate with a slice of pizza and put it on his tray. The drinks dispenser was different than the one at his old school and he over-filled his cup.

"Oops," said Rodney when he saw David put the brimming cup on his tray. Then he rammed his tray against David's so that the drink sloshed over onto David's pizza. Rodney made big eyes. "Sorrrrrry." He and the other boy laughed again.

David said nothing.

"Madeleine? Come here, please," Mrs. Hallowell said.

A girl stood up. She was small as a second-grader, scrawny-skinny with long blond hair. She wore a dress made of T-shirt material that had bunnies on the front, like little kids wore. On one of her knees there were three Band-Aids, and on the other, two. They had stars on them.

"Since you've already finished your project, Madeleine," Mrs. Hallowell said, "will you sit here with David and help him with his workbook?"

Yikes! David was thinking. *Save me from this!*

The girl brought a chair over and set it next to David's. Rodney, across from him, cracked up. The girl ignored him. She had really pale skin and sores on her fingers. She looked six years old.

Desperate not to need the girl's help, David bent over his workbook and concentrated hard.

"That's wrong," she said, and pointed to the third question.

"I-I know it is."

"You want the answer? It's sixty-four."

"I-I know it. I just didn't write it down. I-I don't need any help," he said, erasing what he had and putting down 64.

She shrugged. "Nothing off me, if you don't want help. I was just saying."

At recess David wandered around, deep in thought. What if he ran away? Lily was only eleven when she'd started doing it. Maybe Lily wasn't so stupid after all. Maybe she'd simply felt like he did now, like she'd gotten stuck in the worst place in the world.

"Hey, you!"

David looked up.

Rodney was standing at the corner of the school building. There were two other boys from his class too, although David couldn't remember their names. The three of them surrounded David.

One boy had frizzy blond hair, very light-colored and curled so tightly it looked like sheep's wool. He stuck his face up so close to David's that their noses almost touched. His breath stank of Doritos.

"We're boss and you're not," he said. "Got it?"

David didn't answer.

"And we don't like retards."

David tried to move away.

"Nobody said you could go," Rodney said. "You got to say 'boss' first. To show you know who's boss around here."

David didn't say anything.

"B-b-b-boss!" Sheep Hair said, mimicking David's stutter. He sprayed Doritos spit when he did it.

Before the sheep-haired kid knew what was coming, David slammed his fist into the boy's face. Hard. Because the one thing David *was* good at was fighting. You had to be, if you were no good at running.

Rodney started screaming, "Mr. Dawson! Mr. Dawson!" He tore off across the playground. "Mr. Dawson, that new kid hit Brandon!"

So that's how David ended up in the principal's office on his very first day at a new school.

"Me and Matt and Brandon were just standing

around," Rodney said, "and he says, 'I was the boss at my old school and I'm going to be boss here too. You say I'm boss or I'll give you a bloody nose.'"

Mr. Dawson took David by the shirt collar and marched him off to the principal's office.

"Every start is a fresh start, young man," Mr. Dawson said to him, once the door to his office was closed. "From what I can tell, you are a boy badly in need of a fresh start." He indicated a thick file lying on the corner of his desk.

"I-I need the bathroom," David replied.

Mr. Dawson rolled his eyes impatiently. "You can just wait. Because I want to get this straight with you right now, young man. Hitting is *not* an appropriate way to solve problems in this school."

"*P-please?* I've really got to go."

Mr. Dawson made a stifled snorty noise like a horse with its nose in a bucket. "Okay, but hurry. I'll give you exactly two minutes." He pointed to his watch.

David shot out of the office. Recess had already ended, so everyone else was back in their classes. Loping down the cool, dark, empty hallway, David didn't turn into the boys' restroom when he came to the end. Instead he just kept going. Straight out the door.

THREE

David ran until he was so out of breath he had to stop. Uncertain where he was, he looked around as he stood panting. In the city all the roads had four lanes and noisy traffic, day and night. On this street there were no cars at all except for parked ones. Probably because the streets here were so worn out. He was used to broad black asphalt roads with white lines painted on them, but here the streets looked like they were made of cement. This one had big cracks all across it, patched up with something black, as if someone had used a giant tube of black glue.

At the far end of the street, David could see open countryside. David had never really been in the country before. He'd seen it from cars, of course, but it was simply something that had filled up space between where he was going and where he'd come from.

Breath back, he took off at an easy lope toward the open land in the distance. The sidewalk soon dead-ended into a winter-ragged field. A barbed-wire fence ran across the end of the pavement. Beyond was rough pastureland.

After slipping through the strands of barbed wire, David walked cautiously over the uneven ground, feeling exposed there in the open. When he spied a small gully, David slithered down the embankment. At the bottom was a tiny creek lacing through rocks and crumpled brown reeds, so David followed it, using the tip of his shoe to break through the ice, thin and crackly as spun sugar.

Farther along, he came across an enormous boulder that looked a little like a great gray chair. A throne. David clambered up on top of it and sat down.

When he was little and still living at the Soames', Mom Soames had once read him a story about a powerful king named Arthur, who was guarded by a wizard and had a band of loyal knights. It was a book from the library, so David hadn't been able to keep it very long, but he'd liked the story so well, he'd made Mom Soames read it until she finally said she was grateful she had to take the book back.

He never got to see the book again, which was a pity because he would have liked to have heard the story even more times, especially the part about King Arthur, who had been a foster child too who no one knew was actually a king until the day he'd pulled the sword from the stone. Consequently David had had to make do with his imagination. Mostly he'd pretended King Arthur was really his dad and was looking for him and someday he'd find

David and take him home to the castle, but other times David had pretended he was King Arthur himself. It was only a little kid's game, of course, just make believe, but even now he felt good, remembering it.

From his rock throne, David surveyed the countryside. It was late February, so everything was still colored brown and yellow and gray. Winter colors. They were beautiful together, David thought. He liked the way the brown grass bent forward like tousled hair over the rim of the gully. Above, the sky was pale blue and cloudless.

As he looked around from his high vantage point, David noticed a small building off through a tangle of scraggly trees by the creek. It was old and rundown and nearly invisible in the willowy undergrowth.

Sliding off the rock, David picked his way through the brush to investigate. It was just a shed. It had been painted barn red once but the color was now faded to rust. There was a small, four-paned window with two of the panes broken out and a door on loose, creaky hinges.

Gripping the edge of the door with his fingertips, David managed to get it open. He peered in. The floor was covered with bits of old, dusty straw, as if animals had been kept in there once. Entering, he stepped carefully in case whatever had been in there had pooped on the floor. The ceiling was low. If he stretched up, he could touch it with his fingertips.

Cool! This place could be fixed up. If he had a hammer and some nails, he could repair the door. If he had a broom, he could get rid of the straw. He pulled cobwebs away from the remaining glass on the window. This would make such a great den! David grinned.

The excitement lasted all the way back to Granny's.

"Well, mercy, you've decided to come back after all!" Granny exclaimed when David opened the door.

All the horrible things that had happened at school came rushing back. Not that he'd forgotten exactly about the fight or running out on Mr. Dawson, but he'd managed to squish them down into a corner of his mind, sort of the way you cram the little jack-in-the-box puppet back into his box. And now, just like a jack-in-the-box, they jumped back out so suddenly that David felt his heartbeat rushing in his ears.

"What's the idea of going off like that?" Granny asked. She had been frying pork chops in a pan and had a spatula in her hand. She folded her arms across her chest, but still had hold of the spatula. "Didn't you think I'd be worried?"

David lowered his head.

"Mr. Dawson calls here and says you're gone. I'm beside myself, not knowing *where* you are. This makes me feel very frightened, because you've just come and I'm scared you'll get lost. I was very worried."

David hadn't meant that. He hadn't realized she'd feel scared.

"And I'm sure there must be your side of what happened at school," she said, and her voice had a coming-down-soft kind of sound to it, like maybe she really did think that and wasn't saying it to cover up how mad she was. "I'm sure there must be a reason. People don't run off for no reason at all. So I'm not angry. I just want to know what made you feel things were so bad you had to run away from them."

David couldn't get his mouth to form words, so he just kept his head down.

"No, you look at me. You raise your head and say, 'I'm just as good as that person I'm talking to, so I don't got to look down at the dirt.' You tell yourself that. Then you tell me where you been. Because we don't run away from things in this house. And we don't get in fights. If we got problems around here, we use our voices, not our fists. And we own up to where we been."

David put his hands over his ears.

Granny didn't lecture anymore and she didn't get fed up because David couldn't find the words, although there were a lot of long pauses at dinner, like she was waiting. She just said again that wasn't the way things got done in her house and that there wasn't any choice but to go back to school the next day and own up.

Mr. Dawson, however, had saved his lecture about how you didn't fight on the playground. When Granny dragged David to school the next day, like a bad puppy returning to obedience class, Mr. Dawson wagged his finger and talked about the detention room and how David, once he was done eating, was going to be spending his lunch hour there for four days.

David wanted to say, "What about Rodney and that sheep-haired kid? Did they get detention too?" But he didn't because he couldn't get his mouth to say the words. Instead, he looked at the pattern of the wood grain on the countertop. Mr. Dawson was going on about how it was a bad thing that a boy would get detention after only one day in school. David imagined the wood grain was really the paths of dried-up rivers around little islands. Maybe on some distant planet.

That day David started with Mrs. Chisholm. She was the resource teacher, which was a polite way, David knew, to say she taught stupid kids like him. Mrs. Chisholm's room was down the hall from Mrs. Hallowell's and it was more like a storeroom than a classroom because it was almost full of metal cabinets. Mrs. Chisholm was sitting at a round table by the window and asked David to sit down beside her.

"It says you have dyspraxia," she said, pointing to a file she had open in front of her.

"Challenged." That's how his teacher in the other school put it. "David is challenged." Which made it sound like he was planning to climb Mount Everest or something, when all she really meant was that nothing in his body seemed to work as well as it did in anybody else's.

"Can you tell me what kind of problems you're having?" Mrs. Chisholm asked.

Where to start? David thought. Should he tell her he couldn't run very well? Or about how hard he found writing? Or that he stuttered?

David just gave a shrug and hoped that explained everything, because, really, she had it all written down in front of her. It would say there what a failure he was.

"Do you have trouble talking? Saying words?" she asked.

David nodded.

"And reading and math? Academic things?" she asked.

David's shoulders sagged. Why didn't she ask him what he did well instead? That'd take no time at all to tell, because there wasn't anything.

Mrs. Chisholm wanted him to finish the math paper before going outside to recess, so by the time David got out, everyone else was already there.

He checked for where Rodney and the sheep-haired kid were. They were together on the far side of the playground. Rodney was fooling around with a ball, and a bunch of kids were gathered, watching. Rodney was right about one thing. He was boss in their class. Only two days there and David could tell that was true. Kids were always running after him, wanting to do stuff with him, wanting to be friends with him. Probably because that was a lot wiser than being his enemy.

Seeing two other boys from his class throwing a football back and forth on the playing field, David went in that direction. One of the boys was named Allan and seemed okay. David couldn't remember the other boy's name. Coming to the grassy edge of the asphalt, David stopped and watched them. Allan and the other boy didn't seem to notice him. David didn't think he should ask to join in, because he was so bad at catching things.

How did people make friends? Everyone else made it look so easy. David had often tried hanging around on the edges of groups in hopes someone might notice and talk to him, someone who would give him time to answer. Other times he'd tried to do something nice, just to let the kid know he'd like to be friends. But nothing ever happened. Sometimes they made him fight, like the kids yesterday, but mostly everyone ignored him, like he wasn't even there.

Wearily David turned and wandered back toward the school building. At about Number 3 on the Very Worst Things list was having no friends. Number 4 was all the work you had to go to so that no one knew you cared.

FOUR

When the bell rang at the end of the day, David put on his backpack and shot out of the school yard and down the street. In the morning he had packed things to clean the shed with: a rag to wipe the window, some bits of cardboard to block the winter wind from coming through the broken panes, and a whisk broom. He'd wanted to take a real broom, because that's what he needed to sweep out all the leaves and moldy hay, but a broom wasn't exactly something you could sneak into your backpack.

He was already around the corner from the school when suddenly someone grabbed hold of his backpack from behind and pushed him to the ground. David rolled over to see Rodney, the sheep-haired boy, and another sheepy-looking boy about thirteen or fourteen.

"You're going to get a lesson, kid," the older boy said. "Nobody gets away beating up my brother."

"Yeah, you stupid retard," Brandon said, and danced

around, punching the air. "Teach him, Wesley."

David couldn't see any choice but to hit first before he got hit, because Wesley was bigger. So he socked Wesley right in the jaw, hard as he could. Wesley grunted and stumbled, but then he came right back on David.

After that, there was no chance. Wesley punched him and David fell. Brandon pulled David's backpack off and flung the contents around while Wesley and Rodney attacked him.

When David had lived at the Hortons', there'd been a teenage kid there who knew how to fight and he'd taught David stuff, but none of it worked two against one. David flailed more than punched. All he wanted to do was get up off the ground so he'd have a fair chance, but he couldn't. The boys kept pummeling him until finally he lay panting in the dirt and stopped struggling. Then they got up, dusted themselves down like they'd finished really filthy work, and started to walk away. Only Rodney paused to look back. "You *girl*," he said. Then he spit at David.

David staggered to his feet, moving carefully to see what hurt. He collected up the stuff that had been thrown out of his backpack and started walking toward the field at the end of the street. Feeling hurt and angry and stupid, he squeezed through the barbed-wire fence and shuffled off across the dried, broken winter grass. The gully came up on his right but he didn't turn down there. Instead, he just kept walking.

Mostly David felt mad. He didn't know why really, but

it was a hideous gnawing, like a rat inside his head. Coming up to the side of a small hummock, David started picking up stones and throwing them. Hard. Heat-seeking missiles, that's what they were. Not because there was anything hot out there for them to seek, but just because the words sounded dangerous. He threw rocks so hard his shoulder hurt.

On the other side of the knoll, shaggy clumps of sagebrush humped up above the grass like ghosts in ill-fitting sheets. He kicked at one bush. Once he'd seen pictures on TV of how missiles, hidden out in barren parts of the country in underground silos, would rise up through secret doors and shoot out, seeking the enemy when the president pressed a red button. David imagined metal doors pulling back somewhere inside him and missiles shooting out of his toes as he kicked the sagebrush.

Whoosh. Down his leg. Out his toes. Off to blow up Wesley's head. Kicking was the only way to get the missiles out so that they didn't explode inside, so that there wouldn't be a nuclear explosion in the silo, destroying him. David kicked the sagebrush so hard that tiny gray-green leaves scattered in an explosion of their own.

Unexpectedly, a big bird flew up from behind one clump for sagebrush when David kicked it. At first David didn't see what kind of bird it was, but it didn't fly far. It came back toward him and landed on the ground.

An owl? He'd never seen an owl up close before, but this definitely was one. And it didn't like him being there. It fluttered and squawked, coming toward him, then backing off, then coming again.

Just like Rodney, all cocky and full of fancy footwork. Someone had said Rodney took dancing lessons. Any other boy would have been embarrassed about knowing how to dance, but Rodney used it to show off. To show he was boss, because no one would dare make fun of him for it.

Stupid bird, dancing like Rodney. David picked up a stone and threw it at the owl. The owl let out a loud whirring noise and rose into the air.

Within moments, however, it was back, landing on the ground nearby. It started up its stupid shuffling dance once more. David picked up more stones and threw them. He almost hit the bird with the second one.

As he moved toward the bird, he suddenly saw why it wouldn't fly away. There on the ground beneath the sagebrush was a shabby little nest with two eggs in it. With his anger still as treacherous and confined as those hidden missiles, all he wanted to do was wreck it.

"I-I'll show you who's b-boss!" David screamed at the bird and kicked the ragged little nest. One egg smashed with a satisfying crack. Chasing the owl down the slope, he threw stones at it until it finally circled up into the air and flew away.

For a small moment David felt a heat-seeking-missiles-hitting-their-target kind of good. But it disappeared, leaving him with a tired, soggy sort of feeling, as if someone had dumped a pan of dirty dishwater over him.

Wearily he turned and climbed back up the rise to find

where the nest had been. It was stupid of the owl to build its nest on the ground. He hadn't known they did that. Maybe it was a retarded owl.

The scuffed-up soil led him back to where the nest had been. The second egg had rolled under the sagebrush. It was small and white, looking like an ordinary egg, except maybe a little rounder. David picked it up. Probably it *was* a retarded owl that had laid its eggs on the ground instead of up in a tree where birds belonged. Probably this was a retarded egg.

Not knowing what else to do with the egg, David put it into his pocket. Then he started down the slope. He might as well stop by the shed. He had, after all, come all this way.

Slipping down into the gully and working his way along the creek to the shed, David creaked open the door and went inside. Removing his backpack, he unzipped it and started to take out the things he'd brought to fix the shed up.

"What are you doing here?"

Startled, David whirled around.

There in the doorway stood that girl from his class. The one who looked about six. Madeleine.

"What are you doing here?" she asked again, and not in a little-girl way. It was a demand.

"Wh-what are *you* doing here? Th-this is my place."

"No, it's not."

"Y-yes it is."

"No, it's not."

27

"I-I found it. That's my cardboard there. I-I'm fixing up the window."

She wasn't a very pretty girl. Her features were flat and ordinary. Her blond hair was thin and fine, not the sort of hair that should be so long. The ends were straggly and uneven. Her eyes were a washed-out sort of green and her skin was pale, like she spent all her time indoors.

David was wishing very much that she was indoors right now.

"You shouldn't be here," she said matter-of-factly. "This isn't your land. It belongs to my dad and therefore it belongs to me, and you're trespassing."

David knew he could beat her up easily, if that's what she wanted, because she hardly came up to his shoulders. He didn't think she'd try. She didn't look like she would. But she didn't look like she was going to go away either.

"I said, you *shouldn't* be here. It's not your land."

David brought his shoulders up in a hump around his neck. This made him look really fierce. He practiced it a lot in front of the mirror to get the look just right and he did it now, hoping she might be a sensible little girl and get scared and run home.

"I'll get my dad, if you don't listen to me," she said, not paying any attention to how dangerous he looked. "If I tell him you were fooling around on our property, he'll call the police."

David didn't want that. If someone called the police on him and Mrs. Mellor found out . . . But he didn't want to leave the shed, either. If her stupid dad owned it, he didn't know how to take care of it. It was falling apart. Practically a ruin. David was at least going to make some use of it. Not *hurt* it any. Frustrated, he jammed his hands into his pockets.

He felt the egg.

It occurred to him that if he showed her the egg, she might forget about getting her dad. Probably she'd never seen an owl egg up close. Probably she'd think it was cool he had one.

Taking it from his pocket, David opened his hand so that she could see it.

"What's that?" she asked.

"An egg."

"I can *see* it's an egg. I've got eyes. But how come you've got an egg in your pocket?"

"I-it's an owl egg."

David could tell this impressed her. She came closer. "Can I see it?" she asked.

David closed his fingers over it.

"Please?"

He opened his hand flat.

Madeleine picked it up. "Where did you find an owl's egg?"

"I-I was out walking and this owl flew up."

"You shouldn't have touched it, you know. The mother won't go back to a nest, once you've touched the eggs. They'll just be left to die. Were there others?" she asked.

David shook his head.

She turned the egg over gently. "Can I have it?"

"N-no, it's mine."

"What are you going to do with it?" She kept hold of it, her grubby little fingers wrapped around the white shell.

"I-it's mine. I found it."

"Yeah, but you're not going to do anything with it. If I keep it, I can hatch it."

"L-like how?"

"My dad's got an old kerosene incubator. I could set it up and put the egg in and hatch it."

"M-Madeleine, give it to me."

"Don't call me that. Nobody calls me Madeleine."

"The t-teacher does."

"Well, she's nobody, huh?" she said, and gave him a little grin. "If you want to be my friend, you got to call me Mab."

Who had said anything about wanting to be friends? All David wanted was his egg back.

"You know who Mab is?" she asked. "Mab is queen of the fairies. That's me!" She laughed.

David stared at her. This was definitely *not* the kind of thing you told people when you were in the fifth grade. Not that you were queen of the fairies.

She held the egg against her chest and said, "So, can I have it?"

"*N-no*. It's mine. *I* found it."

"Yeah, on my dad's land," she replied, showing no sign of giving the egg back.

David sighed heavily. He didn't want to fight her for it,

because that would probably break the egg and then where would they be? But he would never have let her hold it if he'd thought she was going to steal it from him.

"Besides, what are *you* going to do with it?" Mab asked. "I can hatch it. You can't. You'll just keep it until it goes rotten and what do you want a rotten egg for?"

They stood a long moment, staring at each other.

"Well, look," Mab said at last in a rather fed-up voice, "I *suppose* you could help me."

"H-help you what?"

"Hatch the egg, stupid."

FIVE

"How old are you?" David asked as Mab led him into the barn.

"Nine. Well, almost nine." She clambered up over a galvanized feed bin to reach the incubator. It was an old, bulky, shabby-looking metal box with a tiny glass window on top and rust along the corners. "You have to put kerosene in there to make it run," she said, fingering the lid. "But that's okay because there isn't any electricity in the shed anyhow."

"Almost nine? Does that mean eight?" David asked. "How come you're in the fifth grade if you're only eight?"

"I got skipped ahead. Twice. Come on. We got to clean this up. I'll show you where to get water."

"Are you a genius?"

"Who knows?" Mab replied offhandedly, as if it weren't something worth wondering about.

"*Are* you?" David persisted because he wanted to know. He'd never met a real genius.

"Do you do nothing but ask stupid questions?" she replied in a crabby tone. "I'm like everybody else. Normal for me. Normal, but different. Okay?" She looked over at David. "I mean, it's like if I asked you how come you stutter. How would that make you feel?"

"P-people ask me that all the time."

"Yeah, well, people ask me this all the time too, and I hate it. Besides, we need to concentrate on this if we're going to get it set up before it gets too late."

David followed her into another room in the barn. "D-do you really think we could hatch this?" In his pocket he put his hand around the egg, fingering it gently.

"I've hatched lots of other eggs before," Mab replied. "Mostly chicken eggs, but I once hatched some pheasants. And a goose. The goose was hard to do."

"W-what would we do with an owl?"

Mab shrugged. "Just hatch it. See what happens. I like to do stuff just to see what happens."

It took both of them to carry the incubator out to the shed. It wasn't big but it was awkward; plus, Mab had already put the kerosene in, so it was heavy.

David kept glancing at her as they walked. Was she really a genius? Even though he'd been in the class only a couple of days, he'd already figured out she was the smartest kid, but there was still a big difference between being smart and being a genius. She didn't look anything like David expected a genius to look. She looked completely ordinary.

But she was *eight*?

The hardest part of getting the incubator to the shed was going down into the gully without tipping it so that the kerosene spilled out. David went first because he was so much taller, and then took the weight of it while Mab jumped down beside him.

"Let's put it over here," she said once they were inside the shed. "That way the flame won't get blown out when we open the door."

Pulling a small box of matches out of her pocket, she knelt down, slid open the box, and took out a match. "See, you light it here. Then you make the flame bigger or smaller by turning this handle thing."

The only eight-year-olds David had known who lit matches were the kind who set fire to things for fun. Mab, though, lit the match matter-of-factly and put it into the small hole at the side of the incubator. There was a soft *whoof* and a sharp, unfamiliar smell.

"We've got to look up how hot it needs to be," Mab said.

"Why do we do that?"

"Because it's got to be the right temperature, stupid. Too low and it won't hatch. Too high and it'll cook the egg, and we don't want that!" She grinned. "Here. Give it to me." Mab held her hand out.

David took the owl egg from his pocket. Mab gently set it in the incubator. She closed the lid.

"The other thing we need to look up is how long it's going to take. You want to research that? I'll try to find out about the temperature."

Research? Panic hit David. Here was a girl genius who could probably read college textbooks. How would he admit he couldn't even read comics?

"I-I don't have any books on owls," David said quickly.

"Look it up on the Internet."

"I-I don't have a computer."

"Well, how about the library then?" From the tone of her voice, David could tell she thought even a moron would have figured that one out. Then she softened a bit. "I mean, I'd go to the library myself, but I have to take the school bus home. You live in town, so it's more fair if you go."

David's heart was doing the Nervous Tango inside his chest.

Mab's shoulders dropped in exasperation. "Am I going to have to do all the work here? Can't you even try to help? What about the school library?"

School! What was going to happen to him if Rodney or Brandon saw him hanging out with some eight-year-old *girl?*

"M-maybe it's better not to do it at school. M-maybe we should keep this a secret," David suggested.

"How come?" Mab asked.

"We wouldn't want anyone to hurt the egg. If-if they found out."

"I don't think anyone would really come out here," Mab said.

"I-I did, didn't I? I-I think we better pretend we don't know each other. Just to be on the safe side."

35

Mab tipped her head to one side and gave him a funny look. David felt bad for lying to her, but she was probably grateful for not having to be seen with the stupid kid who stuttered.

"I-I better go," David said. "I-it's getting really late."

"So, you gonna come tomorrow?"

"How come?"

"We need to take care of this every day."

David raised his eyebrows.

"I mean, only if you want to. But it *is* your egg. I don't want you to think I was trying to steal it off you or anything. I just didn't want to see it wasted, because I thought this could be fun," she said. "But you don't have to come. I'm happy to do it myself."

"N-no, I'll come."

SIX

The next day at school Mab was cool. She never spoke to him.

David spent more of his time paying attention to her. Her table was right up by the teacher's desk, so he couldn't see her face most of the time, just her pale, straggly hair lying over the back of her sweater, but he learned quite a lot anyway. Like, for instance, there was a smart kids' clique, mostly girls, who sucked up to the teacher and worked on their grades the way some people worked at earning money. Mab wasn't part of it.

He also noticed that when they had to choose partners for English and even he got picked by this kid named Dennis who sat at the next table, Mab was left over. Mrs. Hallowell said, "That's all right, Madeleine, you won't have any trouble doing this by yourself." And Mab didn't seem to mind doing it by herself. In fact, David noticed she did tons of stuff by herself, like playing with a ball at recess or reading a book at lunch instead of talking to anyone.

David felt guilty about telling Mab not to talk to him at school. He wished he didn't feel embarrassed knowing her, but he did. Everybody would think he was really sad if the best he could do for a friend was some kid three years younger than he was.

David also kept an eye on Rodney and Brandon. Brandon sat up front too, so David could see only the back of his woolly head. He wasn't actually so afraid of Brandon. Rodney was another matter. When they were lining up to come in, Rodney caught David's eye. He didn't do anything. He didn't say anything. He just looked at David and David knew it was a boss look. He was just checking David over to make sure David remembered what had happened the afternoon before.

There was a school rule about kids who lived in the country needing to take the school bus, because otherwise they would have to cross the highway. So even though Mab didn't really live that far away at all, she had to wait for the bus. This meant David got to the shed first.

When he arrived, he knelt down and peered through the tiny glass window of the incubator. He couldn't see in very well because the glass was old and had a permanent haze etched into the surface, so he lifted up the lid of the incubator and took the egg out. It was warm. David turned it over in his hand.

"Don't pick it up!"

David was so startled, he nearly dropped the egg.

"Don't you know anything? You'll hurt it doing that,"

Mab said as she pushed closed the door of the shed.

Quickly David put the egg back into the incubator.

"You'll hurt the baby growing inside the egg if you move it around a lot," Mab said in a nicer voice.

"I-I didn't know."

She was lugging a tin container. "I brought this because we've got to refill the kerosene reservoir. What's the temperature?"

There was a long thermometer slotted in behind the flame. He pulled it out of its holder. Truth was, he'd never handled a thermometer like this before and had no idea how to read it, so he just twisted it around in his hands the way he'd seen people do on TV. "It's o-okay."

"What's it say?"

"I-it's the right temperature."

"But *what* temperature?" Mab insisted. "Don't you know how to read it? Give it here."

David said, "I-I need glasses. That's why I can't read it."

"Oh," she replied, and seemed to believe this. Lifting up the thermometer, she peered closely at it. "Hundred and two. I haven't found anything specifically about hatching owls, but I think that's okay. That's what you need for chicks." She slid the thermometer back into its slot.

For a moment both of them leaned over, peering into the incubator.

"What shall we call it?" Mab asked.

"C-call it? It's an egg."

"Yeah, but we can still name it something. Because it's

going to be an owl soon." She grinned at him. Her eyes were little-girl sparkly then, like she was thinking of Barbies or something. "I *love* naming things, don't you?"

Well, not really. Or at least he hadn't given it much thought.

"I think we should call it Bubo. That's Latin for 'owl,'" she said.

"King Arthur."

"Bubo's the scientific name. I looked it up last night."

"N-name him King Arthur."

"It might be a girl. And with Bubo it wouldn't matter. Besides, I like saying it. It sounds funny."

They both leaned over the incubator again. Their heads almost touched, and David could smell the shampoo she used on her hair. "I-I like King Arthur better," he said quietly.

David was already seeing images of this majestic bird, handsome and powerful. And belonging to him.

"I don't think a dinky thing like an egg should have a name like King Arthur," Mab said.

David didn't think a powerful, handsome bird should have a silly-sounding name like Bubo, but he couldn't get the words out before Mab was talking again.

"King Arthur is kind of a magic name, I guess. That'd be good. I like magic names. That's why I'm called Mab."

David wasn't paying attention. In his head he could see the owl out in the open, flying high, his wings wide and silent. A hunter. A killer. Swooping down on prey. Gliding soundlessly through the darkness. Returning to him after the hunt. *His* owl. Returning because it belonged to him.

"Know what?" Mab said. "In the old days when there were knights, they used to train owls to hunt for them. Owls and hawks and falcons. All sorts of birds of prey."

"P-probably King Arthur had an owl."

"He did in the cartoon. Did you see that?"

David shook his head. He wasn't talking about cartoon birds. Or cartoon kings.

"That might have just been made up," Mab said. "Like those birds were in the cartoon Cinderella. They're not in the real fairy tale. I have a book about King Arthur at home, and I don't remember reading anything about owls in it."

"R-really?"

Mab raised an eyebrow. "Yeah, really. I didn't read anything about owls in it. What's so weird about that?"

David hadn't meant that. He'd meant, did she *really* have a King Arthur book at home? Maybe she'd bring it to the shed so that he could look at it. He was going to ask, but he didn't get a chance because Mab was already talking again.

"If you like King Arthur, you should read *Lord of the Rings*. That's a better story, I think. I could lend it to you, if you want, because I got the books for my birthday." Then suddenly her face brightened. "Hey, I know! Let's call him Aragorn! Aragorn is this really cool guy in *Lord of the Rings*. He's a king too, but way cooler. Aragorn would be a perfect name."

No. David did not think some guy he had never heard of was cool. It had to be King Arthur.

David tried to hurry his tongue into the right place to tell Mab this before she started talking, but the thing about Mab was that she talked a lot. And she talked fast. Before David even managed to open his mouth, she was off saying something else.

"You got to read that story. You want to borrow my *Lord of the Rings*? I'll bring it for you tomorrow."

SEVEN

During Monday afternoon recess, David asked the teacher on duty if he could go inside to use the restroom. Once he was finished, he thought maybe he'd go see Mab. She'd had a dentist appointment in the morning, and so she'd stayed in at recess to finish the work she'd missed. Maybe he would talk to her today. He felt bad about ignoring her at school.

When he got near the door of the classroom, David heard another voice inside, so he stopped. There were long, narrow windows on either side of the classroom door. If he was in the right position, he could spy without being seen, so he sidled up.

Rodney.

Mr. Dawson must have given him the chore of taking the weekly news magazine around to the different classrooms, because he was carrying a big box. He went to the back table and started lifting the new magazines out.

Mab had her back to the door, so David couldn't hear

what she was saying, but Rodney got mad. He came across to her table, reached over and pulled the pencil she was using out of her hand.

"Gimme that!" Mab said loudly.

"Oh, did I hear a mouse squeak?" Rodney replied, and cupped his hand to his ear. Then he slipped the pencil crossways through his fingers and slammed his hand down on the table. The pencil broke in two.

"Stop it!" Mab cried.

"You shouldn't be playing with pencils," Rodney replied. "Too dangerous for babies, didn't you know?" With that, he picked up her pencil case and took out her other two pencils and broke them in the same way.

Mab started to cry. David wanted to go in and tell Rodney he better plan on paying for those pencils. He could punch Rodney to the floor so easily. Then Rodney'd be the one who was crying.

But David didn't move. He just stood, watching. Rodney threw Mab's pencil case on the floor, then picked up the box with the news magazines in it and started for the door. Not wanting to be caught spying, David hurried over to his locker on the other side of the hallway and quickly opened it, so that Rodney would think he was just in to get his stuff.

"Hey, retard," Rodney said as he came out of the classroom. He swerved abruptly and banged David's locker door as he passed to make it hit David in the head. David reached up quickly enough to catch it in time and Rodney made a rude gesture with his hand, then disappeared into the next classroom.

David took a couple of steps along the hallways to see into their room again. Mab was just sitting there with her back to the door. She wouldn't be able to do any more work because she didn't have any pencils left.

David would go in and give her one of his pencils. It'd be so unfair if Mab got into trouble with Mrs. Hallowell because she didn't have a pencil to do her work.

David thought this. Truth was, he really, really wanted to do it. But somehow his feet got superglued to the floor, because he couldn't move them. So he stood a while longer thinking about what he wished he could do. Then he turned and went back out onto the playground again.

In the shed after school David tapped on the glass of the incubator with his fingertip. "Hey, K-King Arthur," he whispered. "H-how're you doing?"

A pleasant shiver went through him as he watched the egg. He'd never had a pet before. He'd *always* wanted one. When he lived at the Andersons', they'd had cats. Two of them, named Basket and Blue, although Blue wasn't blue at all. He was a tabby. And Basket was black and white. Man, David had loved those cats. It was like having someone peel off his skin when he'd had to leave them.

"Did you turn the egg?" Mab asked when she came into the shed.

David shook his head.

Carefully Mab lifted the lid off the incubator. "Since you always get here first, you can be the egg turner, if you want."

"How c-come we do that?"

"It keeps the baby growing right. Otherwise it would get lopsided and wouldn't live when it hatched out. In the nest the mother bird turns the egg, but if it's in an incubator, we've got to do it."

David was surprised that there were so many things that had to be done every day—check the temperature, put in more kerosene, refill the water reservoir to keep the humidity right, turn the egg—especially as the egg itself appeared to do nothing except sit there. He found it hard to believe that inside the shell yolk and egg white were transforming into a living owl.

At school David had never managed to find the courage to give Mab one of his pencils, so he thought he'd do it now, mostly just to let her know he knew about Rodney. And he understood. He'd taken one out of his backpack and laid it on the floor by the incubator.

Mab was already talking. "Remember how I was telling you about *Lord of the Rings*? Well, guess what. I've brought you the books." She opened up a grocery bag she'd come in with. "It's actually three books, but they are all part of the same story. Just be sure to read them in order." She started taking them out.

These were *books*. Not kids' books, but *book* books. Mab handed them to him.

What planet had she been on? Didn't she realize he went to Mrs. Chisholm for reading?

"*Here*. Take them."

David accepted one and opened it. There weren't any

pictures. He'd pretty much guessed there wouldn't be any the minute he'd seen the books, but he flipped through anyway, hoping. The print was really dinky.

"What's the matter? Don't you want them?" Mab asked. David could hear she was disappointed. Here she'd planned to do this nice thing for him and now she thought he was being nasty about it.

"I-I don't want to call him Aragorn," David said, because he couldn't think of any other way out of this situation. "I want to call him K-King Arthur."

Mab's features melted into a smile. "That's all right. I don't really care. But even if we don't call him Aragorn, you can still read the books, if you want. I'm sure you'd think it was good. It's a lot like King Arthur."

David reached over and picked up his pencil. "H-here."

Mab's brow drew down in a squiggle. "What's that for?"

"I saw you didn't have any p-pencils this afternoon. After recess," David said in a pointed way.

"Oh. Yeah." There was a drop in her voice.

"You can always use my p-pencils," David said. "Remember that. A-any time."

That night Lily phoned. She said if she kept her privileges, she got to use the phone once a week, and since she didn't have anyone else to phone, she'd phone him. But then she went on to say that if she got a boyfriend, then she was going to phone her boyfriend, like, maybe three times and then David about once. She carried on for about ten minutes going over this confusing, elaborate plan for using her phone privileges.

David had a job getting a word in edgewise. Not that it mattered. He'd wanted to tell Lily about the owl egg, but he knew it wouldn't be something Lily'd be interested in. Besides, if he did, he'd have to tell her about Mab. She'd laugh at him if she found out Mab was only eight. And if he didn't tell her that, then she'd make jokes about Mab's being his girlfriend. She'd never believe him in a million years if he told her Mab was a genius.

So, instead, he said, "G-guess what? I'm reading *Lord of the Rings*."

"What's *Lord of the Rings*?" she asked, which pretty much wrecked that topic.

"They're books."

"Since when did you read books, dummy? Come on. Shock me with something else. What's that lady like you're living with? Your place has got to be better than this stinkhole. I'm gonna be in here, like, two minutes."

"D-don't run away, Lily. That's stupid. It's why you're in there in the f-first place," David replied.

"You know, David, you got it so easy. You don't know what suffering is."

He hated talking to Lily.

"Maybe we could go live with Mom this time," Lily said. "That's what I'm thinking. Mrs. Mellor told me Mom was living in the city now."

Mrs. Mellor hadn't told him that. In fact, the only thing Mrs. Mellor had told him recently about anybody in his family was that the reason Lily hadn't been able to go into a regular foster home with him this time was because she was uncontrollable. He didn't know if she had told Lily that. Possibly not. Some things you didn't tell Lily, because she'd think they were cool, even if nobody else did.

Granny came up the narrow little staircase to his room after the phone call. "Is everything all right?" she asked.

David was lying on his bed. He looked at her hands because he didn't want to look at her face. He found her hands kind of fascinating, the way the skin was all ridged up over the bones and there didn't seem to be any muscles underneath. They really did look like bird feet to him.

"I expect you miss your family a lot," she said in a gentle voice. "It must be so hard coming here all by yourself, without your sister."

Don't say dopey stuff to me, he was thinking, because he knew he'd cry. Using ESP, David tried to will her to go back downstairs.

She didn't. This called for a different tactic.

"C-can I ask you something?" David said.

"Yes, of course you can. You can always ask things in this house."

"W-w-well . . ."

Granny looked at him expectantly.

"D-do you know what *Lord of the Rings* is about?"

EIGHT

Mab wasn't the kind of kid who let things drop. The next afternoon when she came to the shed, she had that grocery bag with her again and *another* book. "Here," she said, "I brought you this, because I guess this is what you really wanted."

It didn't look like anything David really wanted. In fact, it looked totally boring. It was an old, chunky book with a plain blue cover. The dust jacket was missing, so David didn't have a clue what it was about.

He cracked it open. On the first page was very weird writing on what looked like a kind of shield with tall, rather ugly angels on either side. It wasn't a picture book, but there were pictures in it. They were old-fashioned black-and-white line drawings, feathery and detailed, of strange-looking women with hair down to their heels and crowns on their heads, of men in suits of armor, and of strong, long-maned horses.

"Is it K-King Arthur?" David asked.

50

"Are you blind or something? Of course it's King Arthur. It says right there." Mab took the book out of his hands and upended it to show him the spine.

David grabbed the book back. "L-let me look at it."

This wasn't the book he remembered. Not at all. He remembered a kid's storybook. This was like an adult book, even with the pictures. He looked through for one he could recognize, like Arthur pulling the sword from the stone.

"You can't read, can you?" Mab said.

"I-I can so."

"That's how come you didn't know what it was, isn't it? You can't read at all."

"I-I-I can so read. I-I just don't have my glasses."

"You're making that up."

"I-I-I *am* not."

"That's a lie. Because if you needed glasses so much, your folks would get them for you."

"I-I don't live with my folks."

Mab's eyes widened. "Who do you live with then, if you don't live with your folks?"

"My foster mother."

"What's a foster mother?"

Now *she* was asking stupid questions. If she was so smart, why didn't she know the answer to that? *He'd* known what a foster mother was for as long as he could remember, and he was no girl genius. He would have told her that if he could have gotten his tongue to work fast enough.

Mab reached over and took the book out of his hands. "The truth is, you can't read."

All these years since he'd seen King Arthur and now this snotty girl was going to take it away just because she thought he was stupid. Just to show him she was better than him, even though she was smaller and younger. Just to make sure he knew that wasn't a book for kids like him. David clenched both fists and raised them menacingly.

"Wow, don't get so mad," Mab said.

"G-give me the book."

"It is my book, after all, and not yours, so don't speak to me like that. I don't have to give it to you if I don't want."

"I-I know something about you too," David said angrily.

"And I think if you're going to be so hotheaded, you can just get out of here. I don't want you here."

"N-nobody likes you. You haven't got any friends. The k-kids at school pick on you. I know. I-I've seen. So, you're not so hot. And you're ch-chicken. At least nobody breaks *my* pencils. I-I stand up for myself." With that, David turned and stormed out of the shed.

By the time David reached Granny's, he felt miserable. What was the point of making friends if they were going to be mean to you? He clambered up the narrow stairs to his room and slammed the door.

Dinnertime came and David didn't want to go down-stairs. He lay on his bed with the pillow over his head. Maybe he would smother. He'd heard on the radio once where a woman accidentally smothered herself when she was sleeping because she put a pillow over her head. Maybe that would happen now. He wished it would.

Granny came up the stairs. She was wearing a pink-and-white apron with an odd pattern on it that looked like antennas and satellites to David. She was the only woman he'd ever known who wore an apron. It made her look old-fashioned.

"What's the matter?" she asked.

"I-I *hate* it here," David muttered.

"What's happened?"

"It's so stupid here. Everything's stupid."

"Like what, for example?" Granny sat down on the edge of the bed. She had gray curly hair that looked really stylish when she first brushed it in the morning, but by evening it always looked like a cat had been sleeping there. She patted it down with one hand as she talked.

David turned away.

"Tell me what happened," she said when David didn't speak.

He didn't answer.

"You'll find it helps to put words to things," she said, and reached a hand out. David pulled away.

Silence.

"M-my friend Mab, the one from school . . . only she's not my f-friend anymore."

"Why? What did she do?"

"C-called me names. I-I *hate* it here. I-I wish I was back in the city."

"No wonder you're mad. I'd be angry too, if my friend called me names," Granny said. "But maybe it was a misunderstanding. Sometimes that happens. Other times, we say things when we're hurt that we don't mean. Maybe Mab was feeling angry too."

"Sh-she wasn't. She knew what she was saying."

"Well, I'll save you some dinner. Maybe you'll feel hungry later on." She leaned over and patted his hip. David didn't bother to pull away. He let her pat, even though it felt dorky.

After Granny left, David lay in the quiet dusk of his bedroom. He knew he shouldn't have said that to Mab about her getting picked on and having no friends. He didn't either, so who was he to say anything?

But *she* started it.

His stomach felt heavy, like he'd swallowed a wet towel. Truth was, he *couldn't* read. She was saying facts, not calling names.

His thoughts wandered to the King Arthur book. He tried to remember the pictures. They'd been drawn in such fine, spidery lines that they needed careful looking at to see all the details. And he'd hardly had a glimpse.

It was easy enough to avoid Mab at school the next day because they didn't hang out together anyway. Outside at recess and lunch break, David leaned against the wall of the school by the basketball court so that he wouldn't see Mab playing with her ball over by the door. Inside, he concentrated on his work. In fact, he worked so hard when he was in Mrs. Chisholm's room for reading that she commented on it and gave him an extra tick for his chart.

Nonetheless, he couldn't get his mind off their fight. Even if he couldn't see Mab, she was still bugging him in his head. What if they couldn't make it up? Was this the end of things? What about the egg? It was *his* egg, not Mab's. But it was in her incubator. Would she still let him use it? What if he went out to the shed and she got mad about it? But what would happen to King Arthur, if he didn't?

In the end David went. He reckoned if he hurried, he could get there, turn King Arthur over and get away before Mab came.

Pushing the door open, David slipped in and lifted the lid of the incubator. Carefully he rolled the egg over to its other side. As he was getting up, he noticed the grocery bag lying on the floor in the corner of the shed. Going over, David picked it up. Inside was the King Arthur book.

On the spine the lettering was in silver. Running his finger over the letters, David felt how they sank into the binding. Sitting down cross-legged on the floor, he opened the book and paged through for pictures.

They were so strange, those pictures. All the women had narrow, elfish-looking eyes. All the men had shoulder-length hair, and unless they had armor on, they looked like they were walking around in stocking feet, although those were probably some sort of boots. David liked the pictures, however, in spite of their oddness. They had so much detail in them that you could really study them closely and still find more to see.

Instantly he recognized Merlin, the wizard, because even with these extraordinary pictures, Merlin looked just the way David had always pictured him, with a long white beard and hair, and a pointy wizard's hat. Soon he figured out which of the other men was King Arthur.

David was so engrossed that he startled up, dropping the book, when Mab came in. Quickly he bent down, picked it up and put it back into the grocery bag.

There was a sharp pause, prickly as a thistle.

"I-I'm sorry," David said softly. "A-about yesterday afternoon, I mean."

Mab shrugged. She didn't say anything immediately.

"I-I *am* sorry. I mean it. I-I shouldn't have gotten so angry."

"I wasn't trying to make you feel bad," she said, and her voice was a little edgy.

"I-I know."

"I'm not so stupid as you think. I understand what it's like not being able to do stuff other people can," Mab said. "It happens to me too. Only for me it's because I'm younger. Like last spring our class went to the water park for our end-of-school party, and I was the only one who couldn't go on the big water slide, because I wasn't tall enough. I had to stay on the baby slide the whole time, which made me feel really stupid. So I do understand. And I hate people being weird over something I can't do anything about, so I'd never do it to anybody else."

"I-I didn't mean to get so upset. And I-I'm sorry for what I said. I hate bullies, so I shouldn't have said that."

"Yeah, well," Mab replied.

A pause.

"It really doesn't make any difference if you can read or not," Mab said. "I was thinking about that last night and thought, well, we don't *both* need to read. You can do other stuff. Like clean the incubator out. It's really too heavy for me to turn over by myself, but you could do it. And I can do whatever reading we need."

David nodded.

Mab bent down and picked up the grocery bag with the King Arthur book in it.

"F-friends?" David asked.

She nodded and gave a small, tight smile.

Then she took the book out of the bag. "What I was wondering . . . I mean, if you don't think it's stupid . . . but I was wondering, while we wait for the egg to hatch . . . I could read this aloud, if you wanted."

NINE

They never found out exactly how long it took an owl egg to incubate. Mab said it took twenty-one days for a chicken and twenty-eight days for a duck. They put the egg into the incubator on March 2, so Mab reckoned it was going to hatch sometime close to the end of the month.

Every afternoon they went to the shed. David always got there first, turned the egg, and waited for Mab to come. When she did, they took the King Arthur book out of the grocery bag and settled down.

David felt so peaceful sitting in the grungy darkness of the shed and listening to King Arthur stories. Mab's book was very different from the one he remembered. It wasn't a children's book, and even Mab found it hard to read sometimes, because the people in the stories said such strange things, like "I will accept thy gage, Sir Unknown Knight, and when I have overthrown thee, I will yield thee unto those fair ladies for to be their servant."

Truth was, the language was so odd that David often didn't understand exactly what the characters were saying, but it didn't matter. If he lay back and relaxed his hearing, he got used to the sound of it. Even when he didn't understand every word, they still made beautiful pictures in his head.

One afternoon David bought a package of Oreo cookies and brought them to the shed for a treat. Another time he brought a box of graham crackers. Mab said she could get milk for free because her dad had dairy cows and she knew how to take milk out of the pasteurizing vats. She never did, but once she brought a huge bottle of Coke. They laughed because it was funny to drink from such a big bottle. It made David burp. Mab bragged that she knew how to make herself burp, and she showed him. David said that here was one thing he was *loads* better at than she was and she couldn't even touch how good he was. Then he made the loudest, grossest burp he could. Mab laughed so hard Coke came out her nose.

Sometimes they got sidetracked talking and forgot to read. Like once Mab asked, "How long have you been in a foster home?"

"Since I-I was four."

"Wow, that's forever. Do you hate it?"

David shrugged. "I-I don't really remember it any other way."

"But don't you hate being away from your folks?" she asked.

"I don't really remember my f-folks either." He felt like a real freak admitting that. His face grew hot.

Mab was cool about it. She didn't act as if there must have been something horribly wrong with his family to give up their kids or something horribly wrong with him and Lily to make their parents want to give them up. "That must have been scary" is all she said.

Another time David asked, "How come you're called Mab?"

"My mom was taking this course for college and they were studying this poem about Queen Mab. And my mom read it to me. I was, like, five or something.

"See, Mab's this really, really, *really* beautiful fairy. More beautiful than anyone else. And you could see through her. Not transparent exactly. There were different words in the poem, but I don't remember them. But it meant she was super-magic. This one part of the poem said she was so beautiful, everyone was terrified of her. And she rode around in this gorgeous car."

"How c-could something be so beautiful it's terrifying?" David asked.

"I think that can be true. Don't you? That something can be so wonderful or beautiful that you actually feel scared to be around it. Sort of like how you cry sometimes because you're so happy."

"A-and another thing. I-I didn't know fairies rode around in cars."

"I didn't either, to be honest. But she did. It said that in

60

the poem." There was a pause. "Actually," Mab said slowly, "I didn't understand a *lot* of that poem. It was pretty complex. But the car bit is right. I remember, because it surprised me too."

"P-probably it was a Rolls Royce," David said.

"Or a Cadillac. They're fancy."

"P-probably a convertible. That's what I'm going to have, if I get rich."

"Anyway, I just loved that poem," Mab said, "and I used to make up all these plays about Queen Mab and act them out."

"That was like me and K-King Arthur."

"Yeah, except that you probably didn't go around in a pink tutu with one of those silver party crowns on your head all the time," Mab said, and laughed. "My mom thought it was cute. And people just started calling me Mab after that."

It was a good thing they were having fun in the shed, because school certainly wasn't fun. David didn't like Mrs. Hallowell. She looked like she was going to be nice because she was young and pretty, but she was about a hundred years old in her head. All she wanted was for people to sit down, keep quiet, and get good grades. She was *obsessed* with good grades. She was always talking about the school achievement tests, which weren't for another month, and sounded like she was going to take it very personally if hers wasn't the best fifth grade in the district. Worse, she had her Try Harder Club, which was about as dorky as you could get. It wasn't a real club, of course, just an expression she used. Every time David got fed up correcting something, she'd say, "You want to be in the Try Harder Club, don't you?" He wanted to reply with something like, "No, I want to be in the Barf Up Your Breakfast Club," but he never had the courage.

Really, David didn't like the class much either. Mrs. Mellor had told him this was going to be a much better class than his last one. That one had been in a "rough" school, she'd said. This was in a "nice" school and it would be a "nice" class. *Well, sorry to tell you this, Mrs. Mellor, but you're wrong.*

There were only a few kids like Rodney and Brandon whom you had to watch out for all the time, but there were lots more kids who could smile, speak politely, and still treat you like you were something that dropped out of a dog's behind, if you weren't exactly like them. And Mrs. Hallowell never did anything. Maybe she just didn't pay attention, so she didn't realize. Or maybe she was one of those adults who believed in "letting kids work things out for themselves." David didn't know. But he sure never found any of it "nice."

TEN

But in the shed was a completely different world. One afternoon Mab read about how King Arthur received his sword, Excalibur. It was a magic sword, given to him by the Lady of the Lake, who was a mysterious supernatural woman living underwater. And one day she put her hand up out of the water and held out the sword to Arthur, because she recognized that he was the One True King.

Mab read, "'Then King Arthur reached forth and took the sword in his hand and immediately the arm disappeared beneath the water. Then verily his heart swelled with joy and it would burst from his bosom, for Excalibur was a hundred times more beautiful than he had thought possible. Wherefore his heart was nigh to breaking for pure joy at having obtained the magic sword.'"

Those words sounded so mysterious and powerful to David that he asked Mab to read them again. So she did.

David could picture the sword clearly. Huge, glistening,

heavy. He knew that swelling feeling of joy King Arthur had felt because he'd felt it once too.

He was eight and sitting in the office at Social Services waiting to go to a new foster home and this lady who worked there handed him five dollars. She said it was because he sat so quietly. And because he'd told her he was saving up to buy one of those little dogs that have batteries in them so that they can walk around and bark. She just gave him the money. So David knew what happiness was.

On his way home from the shed, David grabbed up a stick and pretended it was Excalibur. He thrust it out ahead of him. He slashed the air with it.

Granny was at the stove when he came into the house. She was making pork chops and the whole kitchen had this fantastic cooking smell. "What are you doing with that big stick?" she asked. "Where are you taking it?"

"I-it's Excalibur!" David replied exuberantly.

"Excalibur? There's a name I haven't heard in years. Where'd you learn that? Are you studying it at school?"

"N-nope," David said, and grinned. "I'm just that smart." And he thundered up the stairs to his bedroom.

David wished the stick was Excalibur. He spent a long time lying on his bed, imagining what it would be like to show up at school with a genuine magic sword. Everyone would crowd around, asking where he got it, and he'd just say, "The Lady of the Lake gave it to me," very casually. Everyone would look astonished and really impressed. Except Rodney would probably ask, "Who's the Lady of the Lake?" He'd be too stupid to know. David smiled. That would be so cool, if it happened.

He should have been getting his homework out, but he lay on his bed, dreaming up pictures of King Arthur and the Lady of the Lake and the sword. David lifted up the stick. Maybe he'd polish it up some. Maybe he'd hang it on his wall. Everybody'd think he just had a stupid stick hanging there. They'd never guess the world had real magic in it.

That night Lily phoned. She wasn't supposed to. She got only one call a week and she said she'd used it Sunday night to phone her boyfriend.

"How'd you get a b-boyfriend?" David asked.

"I met him at the carnival," she replied. "He was running that ride where you stand against the walls and it spins and you stick. Know which one I mean? That one you're always too scared to go on."

David was suspicious. He didn't think there were any carnivals coming around in March. And how had she gone to a carnival anyway?

"He's got a motorbike," Lily said, "and when I get out of here, him and me are going to go riding."

"A-are you making this up?"

"Gad, you're lame. Of course I'm not making it up. You're the one with the freaky imagination, buddy, not me."

David didn't say anything.

"So how's it going there?"

David's head was full of Excalibur and Mab and the owl egg, but he wouldn't dream of telling Lily any of that. She'd think it was so sad that he was still interested in King Arthur and sadder still to have some little girl reading him stories. *At his age.* As for the owl egg, she wouldn't believe him.

"So what's the old lady like?" she asked. "Is she going to keep you? Are you still wetting the bed?"

"I-I-I don't wet the bed. I-I haven't wet the b-bed since I was seven."

"Well, whatever. You know, talking to you is like talking to a wall. Why don't you ever have something interesting happen to you? I should have called my boyfriend."

David didn't say anything.

"Well, gotta go, buddy. Just wanted you to know I haven't forgotten about you. Even if you lead a dull little life. Blood's still thicker than water, hey? Gotta remember that, huh?"

"Yeah," David said, and hung up.

That night Granny came up just before David got into bed. She noticed the stick was lying on the floor. "You still have Excalibur up here, I see."

"I was just fooling around," he said, in case she was going to make fun of him for playing with a stick.

"When I was little," Granny said, "my daddy used to read me the stories of King Arthur and his knights. And

Queen Guinevere. I wasn't sure kids still learned about those kinds of things these days."

Already in his pajamas, David leaned back against the wall beside his bed. He tried to imagine what Granny would have looked like when she was a little girl. He couldn't really.

"Is Mrs. Hallowell reading King Arthur to the class?" she asked.

David shook his head. "N-no."

Granny raised her eyebrows questioningly.

"M-Mab. It's her book." He hesitated. "She's reading it to m-me." The minute he admitted that, he wished he hadn't. Clenching his fingers and his toes, he waited for her to laugh about how freaky it was for two kids to sit around, one reading to the other.

She didn't even react. Instead she said, "Which King Arthur story is your favorite?"

"Excalibur. D-definitely." He wanted to quote to Granny that part about how Arthur's heart was nigh to breaking for pure joy. In his head he could hear the exact words, but there was no way he could get his mouth around them.

He lay down on his bed and stretched his feet out behind where she was sitting. "C-can I ask you something?"

"Yes, of course."

"In K-King Arthur's time, did they really train owls to hunt?"

Granny thought a moment. "I know they trained hawks

and falcons. Hmm. Maybe they trained owls too. I'm not really sure."

David smiled. "I-I'm going to have an owl someday."

"Probably a dog would be better," Granny replied. "Or a cat. They're meant to be pets."

"I-I'm going to have an owl."

ELEVEN

During the third week in March, David came into the shed and noticed that the egg was over toward the side of the incubator and not where he'd set it when he'd turned it the day before. He peered closely. There was a crack in the egg.

"S-something awful's happened," David said when Mab came in. "Somehow the incubator's b-been knocked. It's c-cracked the egg."

Mab knelt down. And then she grinned. "There's nothing wrong. It's starting to hatch. Look there. On this side. See the tiny hole?"

David pressed his face down close. So close, in fact, his breath steamed up the little window.

Wow.

"C-can we take the lid off?"

"No. Don't." She slapped her arm across it protectively. "It'll die. The air makes the shell too hard and then the chick can't break out of it."

Fluttery with excitement, David leaned close again. Through the tiny hole in the shell, he could see the chick inside moving.

King Arthur was in no hurry. For ages David hovered over the incubator, but nothing happened.

"Incubators aren't as good as mother birds," Mab said, "so sometimes the babies take a really long time hatching out."

"Sh-shouldn't we help him?" David asked.

"No. We just got to be patient."

Being patient was almost impossible. David was too keyed up for reading and couldn't sit still that long. He kept checking the incubator.

The egg wobbled occasionally but the hole got no bigger.

"Well, if we're not going to read, we better spend our time figuring out what we're going to do when it hatches," Mab said.

"Wh-what do you mean?"

"Well, we're going to have to feed it, for starters. And it can't live in an incubator."

"H-he can live with me. I-I want to be the one to train him," David said.

"He's going to be a little baby in the beginning. If we want him to grow, we have to feed him. And do you know what owls eat?"

David shrugged. "Owl food? I-I dunno. I haven't thought about it."

"Stuff like dead mice."

"D-dead mice?" He made a face. "Where are we going to get d-dead mice?"

"We've got zillions of live ones in our barns, so I guess we can just set traps for them. But then we're going to have to cut them up. A whole mouse would be too big for a baby bird to swallow. Unless it was a vulture or something." Mab laughed at that. "And I don't think we're hatching a vulture."

David was too busy being grossed out to laugh. "Ewww. We're going to have to c-cut them *up*? I-I don't want to be the one that does that."

"Guess what some mother birds do," Mab replied. "They eat the food first and then throw it up. Right into the baby bird's mouth.

"Ewwww. Yuck. *Yuck!*"

Mab laughed. "Well, it's going to have to eat."

"Well, *you* can throw up dead mice into his mouth then," David said, and shoved her playfully.

Even though they both stayed later than usual, the egg didn't hatch. It did nothing but wobble occasionally, although David could hear a faint tap-tap-tapping coming from the shell if he listened very, very carefully.

Finally Mab had to leave because she'd get into trouble if she was late for supper. David lingered awhile longer, willing King Arthur to break the shell, but it didn't happen. At last David put on his jacket, flung his book bag over his shoulder, and headed home too.

Since it was already six o'clock and Granny'd get angry if he wasn't home soon, David took a different route home because he hoped it would be faster.

"Hey, Buttface!" someone yelled.

"H-h-hey, r-r-retard!" another voice called in a fake stutter. David recognized this one. "L-l-listen. I can talk just like y-y-you." Out from behind a hedge popped Brandon. The other voice belonged to his brother, Wesley.

David ignored them and kept going.

"L-l-look. H-h-he's scared. He's going to r-r-run away," Brandon said, and laughed.

Wesley wasn't going to give David this opportunity. He shot in front of him and blocked his way. "Who said you could come down this street, retard?"

"H-h-he's been to see his g-g-girlfriend," Brandon said. "Haven't you, r-r-retard?" His fake stutter made him sort of bleat the words out. Now he not only looked like a sheep, he sounded like one.

"Been smooching your girlie?" Wesley said, and shoved David's shoulder in a way that would have been playful if they'd been friends. But they weren't friends.

"Shut up," David retorted.

"You think no one knows you're in love with Madeleine Stopes. But you want to be her lover boy." Brandon made kissy noises. "Retard loves Teacher's Pet. What's she do? Give you all the answers? Or do the two of you just go be freaks together?"

This made Wesley laugh. "Bet you get an A plus in Freak class, huh, kid? When you're not attending How to Talk Stupid class." He pushed David hard enough to make him stagger backward.

David pushed back.

"Watch it, kid," Wesley said dismissively, "or I'll beat you up as bad as I did last time."

Wesley took a pack of cigarettes out of his pocket and then fished out a lighter. He was making such a big deal out of doing it, David knew he was just showing off. Wesley held the lighter up near David's face and flicked it.

"S-stop it."

Wesley laughed. "Did I scare you?" Flicking the lighter again, he held it against the strap of David's backpack. The webbing sizzled.

David jerked back. "S-stop it! I mean it!"

"S-s-stop it!" Wesley mimicked. "S-s-s-s-s. You sound like a snake, freakboy." He flicked the lighter again.

Letting the backpack slide down his shoulder a short ways, David grabbed the strap, whirled it around, and hit Wesley. He was quick and Wesley hadn't seen it coming. And David hit hard. Wesley thudded backward on his butt.

Before Wesley could get up, David lifted the pack over his head and hit him again. Then he kicked him hard as he could. Brandon tried to pull David off, but when David whammed the pack around on him, he quickly let go.

It was as if a forest fire were raging through him, because once he got going, David roared on. He kicked and kicked and kicked. Wesley's nose started to bleed. He rolled over on his side and put his hands over his head to protect himself from David's shoes.

"Quit it!" Brandon shouted, dancing just out of David's reach. "You're going to kill him!"

David didn't stop. He couldn't stop. The fire raced through his limbs. When he wasn't kicking, he was lifting the book bag to hit Wesley.

"Stop!" Wesley finally cried out.

Brandon grabbed David again, and David sent him sprawling with one whack of the bag.

Seeing the pack of cigarettes and the lighter on the ground, David stomped frenetically all over them. He smashed the lighter to pieces and kicked the smelly remains at Wesley. With the heel of his shoe, he squashed each cigarette that had fallen out of the pack. "G-go on! G-get out of here!"

Wesley stayed on the ground, his hands over his head.

"You hurt him!" Brandon shouted. His voice had so much hate in it, it was hoarse. "We weren't hurting you any. *We* were just playing. You're *nuts*. You're freaking insane, you are, and now you are going to be in *big* trouble, because I'm going to tell. I'm telling my folks what you did to Wesley and they're going to get the police after you!"

David took off after him. Brandon ran, his sheepy hair waggling. David chased him for maybe half a block, but Brandon was faster. When he darted down between two houses and into someone's backyard, David didn't follow.

He didn't know if it was Brandon's yard or not, but he didn't want to get trapped. Instead he just kept running.

David meant to go home, but he wanted to make sure he got as far away from Brandon and his brother as possible first, even if that meant having to run in the wrong direction to start with. He *knew* they were going to tell. He *would* be in big trouble.

The moment he thought that, actually *thought* about it and didn't just let the thought pass through his head, the forest fire inside him went right out. Abruptly, he stopped running.

If Brandon's family called the police, Mrs. Mellor would find out. If Mrs. Mellor found out he'd been fighting again, she was going to be furious. More than furious. She might well decide he couldn't stay with Granny any longer. Maybe Granny wouldn't even *want* him to stay. That's what happened at the McNicholls'. Between Lily running away all the time and David always getting into fights, the McNicholls decided they couldn't put up with such difficult children. Maybe David would now be sent to a children's home too.

He *wanted* to stay here. Up until that precise moment, David hadn't realized that. He'd been preoccupied with thinking about things like how much he hated having to climb up and down that weird little staircase or how he wished Granny drove a nicer car, and had never stopped to notice he actually liked it here. Now there was no doubt in his mind. It would be horrible if Mrs. Mellor took him away from Granny and Mab and King Arthur.

King Arthur. Oh gosh. Just when it didn't seem possible things could get worse, something worse came along. If Brandon knew about him and Mab being friends, what if he knew about the shed, too? About the incubator?

David's Very Worst Things list got rearranged in a flash, because *here* was a real Very Worst Thing. If Brandon and his brother went to the shed, they'd wreck everything just to get back at David. They'd find the book with its strange words and its feathery black-and-white drawings and they'd think it was all stupid. They'd wreck the shed. They'd kill King Arthur.

The moment David realized that, he knew he couldn't go back to Granny's, no matter what. He had to return to the shed and save everything.

TWELVE

There was no moonlight but there were lots of stars. Once David's eyes had adjusted to the dark, picking his way through the sagebrush back to the shed was an adventure.

David pretended he was Sir Gawain. Mab had just been reading how Sir Gawain and Queen Guinevere had argued. He didn't like her giving him orders, even though she was the queen. Sir Gawain, the story said, was "of proud temper." Like himself, David thought. He was of proud temper too. That sounded a lot better than saying he fought a lot.

Opening the door to the shed, David could see the small, faint light of the kerosene flame that warmed the incubator. He closed the door tightly. Or at least as tightly as he could manage, because the door was pretty rotten. Taking off his belt, David fastened it around a nail and looped it over the doorknob. He tried the door. The belt wouldn't hold for long if someone really pushed against it, but it was the best he could do.

Crossing to the incubator, David knelt down. "K-King Arthur?" he whispered. The egg was just as it had been when he'd left. "You're safe now." David touched the glass softly. "I'll never let anything happen to you. I promise."

David was sorry he hadn't kept Wesley's lighter, because it would have come in handy. He could hardly see anything inside the shed except for the incubator with its pale, smelly flame. Still on his hands and knees, David groped for the King Arthur book. It took a lot of feeling around before he found the grocery bag. He pulled it over beside the incubator.

He tried to look at the book by the light of the flame. This was almost impossible, because the flame was deep down inside the incubator, which meant there wasn't much more than a faint glow through the glass window on top. To see anything, David had to lie on his back and hold the book up over the incubator.

Mab had put a marker in and this tumbled out and hit him on the nose when he opened the book, but he knew where the next story began anyhow.

"'Ch-chapter Ten,'" he said aloud. He knew the word for "chapter" now because it was at the start of every new story. There was a sentence underneath that described what the story was going to be about. "'H-how. King. Arthur. Was. W-w-w . . .'" David had no idea what the next word was. He gave up on that part and skipped to the first line of the story. "'And. Now. Was. Come. The. E-e-ear. Lee. Eeeeerly. *Early*. Fall. Of. The. Y-y-year.'"

This was pretty hard going. David decided to forget about actually reading.

It was hard holding the book that way, up over his head. His arms ached, so he had to rest them occasionally. He paged through, looking for pictures.

There was one picture of a knight called Sir Pellias. They hadn't gotten to the part of the book that told about him, but David loved the picture. In it Sir Pellias was lying asleep on a couch and this woman was leaning over him. She had black hair as long as her floor-length dress and she wore a circle-type crown on her head. She was very, very beautiful and stood over him, gazing down intently on Sir Pellias, asleep. Who was the woman? Why did she gaze so lovingly at him? Maybe she was his mother, who'd been gone a long time and missed him too much and had just come back to find him.

David's arms got too tired, so he lowered the book and sat up. He peered into the incubator. "H-how are you doing in there, King Arthur? About ready to break that shell?"

The egg just sat there.

David felt so hungry that it was like having a wolf roaming around, growling and gnashing its teeth inside his stomach. He stared into the darkness, wondering where he could get some food.

That made David remember why he was there. Not that he had forgotten, of course. Just that while looking at the book, his mind had pushed it aside. Now he remembered too well.

He desperately wished it were afternoon again. When

he'd first seen the hole in the egg and realized King Arthur was hatching, life felt like it couldn't get any better. And now . . . if *only* it could be afternoon again. He'd leave the shed earlier. He'd go home the usual route. Everything would be all right.

A prickly sting came to the back of his eyes, and David didn't bother to fight it down. Who cared? He might as well cry.

Because he wasn't wearing a watch, David had no idea what time it was. There was nothing to do in the dark, so he lay down on the floor beside the incubator. He couldn't sleep. The floor was hard and drafty. The shed got colder. He was *so* hungry. David sat up again, pulled his knees up and rested his arms across them.

All the time he was listening for footsteps.

David plotted how he would defend King Arthur. He'd get some rocks ready, just in case. So he went outside to collect some. The air had gone crackly cold and the frosty grass crinkled as he walked through it. His breath puffed out as wispy as the air rising out of manholes in the city. The moon was out by then but it was high up and only partly full, so that it looked like a distant, half-closed eye.

David carried the rocks into the shed and then went out for a stick he could use as a club. It felt better to move around and do things. He sort of played as he did it, imagining he was Sir Pellias or Sir Gawain and he was on a quest for King Arthur. For a while it was almost fun.

The hardest part was being so hungry. David could

turn his mind away from everything else, but not his stomach. In desperation he went over to the little creek that ran in back of the shed. Bending down, David cupped his hands and drank some of the water. He knew he shouldn't, because more than once Mab had told him cows peed in that water. Probably they pooped in it too, knowing cows. But there were none around right then and the water tasted just fine.

David returned to the shed and fastened the door shut with his belt. He stacked the rocks near the incubator, pulled his jacket close around him, and lay down again, using his backpack as a pillow. This time he fell asleep.

THIRTEEN

David was too cold and uncomfortable to stay
asleep long. Sitting up, he laid his hands on the
incubator lid to warm them. He peered in at
the egg.

There was a crack across the shell.

"W-way to go, King Arthur," he said and leaned closer.
"Now p-push that shell apart."

The egg plainly wobbled but nothing else happened.
The minutes dragged by. David had no idea what time it
was, but the night felt like it was lasting forever. His eyes
grew heavy, so he closed them and leaned his cheek
against the lid of the incubator. It was nice and warm.

Then came a clicking sort of noise. David lifted his
head. The egg was rocking back and forth, going *click,
click, click.* Then it gave one big wobble and abruptly the
end of the shell fell off, and *plop,* out came King Arthur.

David's eyes widened. *King Arthur?*

What lay on the bottom of the incubator did not look

like an owl! It looked like some frail, failed horror-movie creature. It was all wet and had white hair stuck down to a very pink body. Its big bulgy eyes were closed. It had an oversized beak and the most enormous feet. They were so big, they looked like cartoon feet. David could have *drawn* a better owl than this! In a word, it was ugly. Very ugly. Very, very, very ugly.

David peered in closely. Was it even alive? It lay still for a long time, then FLOP! It rose clumsily up and plopped back down again in a heap. It let out a sound that wasn't really a peep or a squawk, but more of a high-pitched "erk." But it never opened its eyes. They seemed stuck shut.

David wished Mab were there. He could have used a girl genius just then. Was this the way baby owls were *supposed* to look? David thought it looked deformed. What if he had not been turning the egg right? Or worse, what if he had damaged it that very first day when he'd kicked it out of the nest? He'd always felt wretched about wrecking the nest; it had been a stupid thing he'd done without thinking. What if it was now his fault that something was wrong with King Arthur?

"P-please be okay," David whispered.

For a long time he watched the owlet. It was certainly alive. It flopped back and forth, trying to get its big feet under it in order to sit up. The wetness disappeared. The white stuff wasn't hair. As it dried, it covered the baby bird's bright pink body with sparse white down.

"You're ugly, K-King Arthur," David murmured. He

smiled. He wanted to lift the lid up and touch the baby owl, but he didn't dare because he knew it would let the heat out. So, he just watched until he finally grew so sleepy that he couldn't keep his eyes open any longer. Lying down on the floor beside the incubator, David fell asleep.

"David? David, are you in there?" The door rattled roughly.

Startled, David jerked awake. It was a man's voice. David picked up one of the rocks.

The man rattled the door again and then went to the window and tried to peer in. David saw it was a policeman.

His heart was in his throat. The only thing he could think to do was run away, but there was no way to get out of the shed. The policeman was at the door again.

David leaned over the incubator to see in. King Arthur was sitting up, looking almost cute, if you were the kind of person to think a ball of scraggly white fluff with bulgy closed eyes and enormous feet was cute. David knew he couldn't run away, even if he did figure a way out of the shed. He had to defend King Arthur.

Putting down the rock, David went to the door and unhooked his belt. The policeman pushed it open.

"Are you all right?" he asked.

David nodded.

"Come on," the policeman said. "You've made a lot of people very worried about you."

"I-I can't go. I-I've got an owl."

"An *owl*?" The policeman went over and peered into the incubator. "Good heavens. Where did this come from?"

"M-my friend and I hatched it."

"Well, your friend can take care of it then. Right now you need to come with me. You've upset a lot of people, running away like that."

"I-I didn't run away. I-I was right here, taking care of him."

"Well, come on now."

David had assumed Brandon's folks had called the police, but in fact Granny had.

"Good gracious!" she cried when she saw David. She opened her arms and pulled him into a big hug. David hadn't expected this, because Granny was not a huggy sort of person.

"I was *so* worried about you," she said. "Lord have mercy, son, you can't imagine what you did to me last night. How could you not come home?"

Mrs. Mellor was sitting in the living room. Normally Granny kept throws over the couch and chairs so they didn't get dirty, but they'd all been taken up. Mrs. Mellor sat primly on the pristine beige couch. She had all her files with her, the ones she brought when she intended to take someone to a new foster home. David started to cry. It happened before he could stop it.

Granny made him sit down in one of the good chairs and then went to see the policeman out. David sat carefully on the very edge because he knew he was dirty.

"I honestly didn't expect this kind of behavior out of

you, David," Mrs. Mellor said. "I didn't think we'd have this problem. Not after Lily. Not after your seeing all the trouble she's gotten into for running away."

"I-I-I *didn't* run away," he said, but his voice was all garbled up with tears. He felt so embarrassed to be crying in front of her.

"I'm sorry, but I can't understand what you're saying. You'll have to speak more clearly."

Granny came back, and when she saw David crying, she put an arm around his shoulder. "This has all been too much, hasn't it? Policemen and everything. I think what you need right now is a good hot bath and then you climb into bed. I bet you've had hardly any sleep at all."

David glanced fearfully over at Mrs. Mellor, who still looked angry. Granny gave him a wad of tissues and he blew his nose.

"Now go on. Go get in the bath and wash all that dirt off you. You look like you spent the night in a haystack," Granny said. "In the meantime, Mrs. Mellor and I will have a little talk."

David ran a bath. He made it much deeper than normal. Granny only ever wanted him to use a little water, because hot water cost money. But this time he ran it so deep he could lay back and get everything under the water at once, except his head. He felt awful. His muscles were heavy. His thoughts were as thick and hard to move around in his head as cold molasses. Worse, he had this deep-down sad feeling that made everything seem impossible. He lay in the water. He didn't wash. He should have, because Granny was right. He was filthy. But David just lay until the water wasn't warm enough. Then he got out, put on his pajamas, and went upstairs to his room. Finding Little Blanket, he pressed it over his eyes. He never bothered to go back downstairs and find out what Mrs. Mellor was going to do.

FOURTEEN

When David awoke, bright sunshine was coming through the small window at the gable end of the room. For a moment he was confused by the sun. His clock said two-thirty. Two-thirty didn't make sense. *Then* he remembered.

David got up and dressed. He still felt tired.

Downstairs Granny was bustling in the kitchen. There was a gigantic chocolate cake sitting on the counter by the stove.

"Good morning!" she said brightly, as if this made sense.

"I-I thought you did for Mrs. Cottlesworth today," he replied.

"I phoned Mrs. Cottlesworth and I told her I couldn't come today. I explained there were problems with my David and she's an understanding lady. Got three boys of her own." Granny smiled. "Look. I made you a cake. How about a piece?"

David looked at her. Granny was not the kind of person who gave you cake when you should be eating sensible food. Maybe she was being extra nice because she knew Mrs. Mellor was going to take him away.

Granny didn't wait for a reply. She cut a huge slice of cake and put it on a plate. Then she poured a glass of milk.

"Wh-what's going to h-happen to me?" David asked fearfully. "Is Mrs. Mellor c-coming back?"

"Later."

David's heart sank.

"Don't look so worried. I said you and me, we'd work things out." Granny put the cake and milk down on the table in front of him. Then she sat down in the other chair. "I told her you'd explain everything and then I'd understand. I told her this wasn't something my David would do without a reason."

My David. Sometimes Granny talked about her husband, who had died a long time ago, and she called him "my Thomas," like he was special property. But she'd never called David that. It sounded nice, but David wasn't sure he believed it. Sometimes people said stuff like that just to make you let your guard down.

"Of course, this means you've got to talk to me," Granny said. "And you've got to tell me the truth."

"I-I didn't run away."

"No, I never thought you did. That's what I told Mrs. Mellor. I said that boy's got no reason for running, so that's not what happened. So why didn't you come home?

Didn't you know it was going to just scare the socks off me?"

David didn't speak at first. There was so much—Brandon and his brother, Rodney, King Arthur, Mab—David didn't know where to start.

Granny didn't look hurried.

"I-I was taking care of King Arthur."

"So, do you care to tell me who King Arthur is?"

And so he did. It was hard. Probably he had never said so many things at once in his whole life, but Granny sat back in the kitchen chair like she didn't really have anything else to do that afternoon.

David told first about King Arthur, about finding the egg and how that led to him and Mab becoming friends. Granny already knew about Mab, of course, because she'd wanted to know where he was spending all his time after school, but David had never told her about the egg.

Then he explained how he had met Brandon and his brother on the way home the night before. He was afraid Granny was going to get mad if he told her he beat up Wesley; so for a moment David thought he'd lie and just say he'd stayed in the shed to make sure the egg hatched okay and not mention Wesley at all. But he still didn't know if Brandon had told his parents. So David figured he'd better tell Granny about the fight, because he was afraid of making things worse if he didn't.

When he was finally finished with the whole story, Granny sat a long time silent. She took the cake knife and scraped up a bit of icing that had fallen on the tablecloth.

At last she said, "Well, it's probably a good thing this came out in the open now, just when your egg hatched. Because your little bird is going to need more care than you can give it in some shed."

There was a long pause.

David looked over. "I-I'm sorry about the fight."

She nodded. "Yes, well, I'm not going to say anything about that. Sometimes when you're on the bottom, folks don't give you no choice but to fight. I understand that. But I am going to say that solving problems with words is a lot better way. More respectful. Of yourself as well as other folks. Any old animal can fight. Shows the world you're a human being, if you use words. And for folks living in this house, that's how we try to do it." She smiled at him. "But I can see you're getting better at it. When you came, I don't think you could have sat down and told me about all this like you just did."

"P-please don't send me away."

"Don't think I heard anyone talking about sending you away," Granny replied. "Have you?"

David looked at her.

"That'd be just a different kind of running away, wouldn't it, if I said I wasn't having boys who fought. To fix them so they stay fixed, problems got to be sorted out. Not run away from." Then she smiled. "Besides, I'd be fat as Tom Kitten if I had to eat all this chocolate cake myself. So there better be a boy here to help me."

David smiled too.

* * *

At four-thirty the doorbell rang. David was only half dressed. He had his sweatpants on but nothing on top. He thought it might be Mrs. Mellor, so he shot upstairs to his room because he didn't want to see her.

He could hear Granny talking to someone in the kitchen and then footsteps on the little staircase. David pulled a sweatshirt over his head.

"Hi." There in the doorway stood Mab.

David looked at her in surprise.

"This is a great room!" Mab said, looking around. "How come you never told me you had a room like this? It's huge. About three times as big as mine. And look at this cool window. You could sit here and spy on everyone in the street."

"Y-yeah."

She looked back at him. "Are you okay?"

"K-King Arthur hatched."

"I know. My dad's gone over to get him. He's going to put him in the barn. We've got a chick brooder there and my dad says that's a better place for him."

David felt sad to hear this. "I-I thought we were going to take care of him."

"We still can. We'll just do it in the barn now. My dad says he won't survive otherwise. In fact, my dad says we're really, really lucky we got him to hatch at all. When I first told him we were doing this, he said then it wouldn't work. He said because we didn't know how old the egg was and because it got carried around, we probably wouldn't be able to hatch it. So obviously King Arthur's a tough little guy."

There was a pause.

"Guess what?" Mab said. "They came and got me out of school today."

"W-who?"

"The police. They came to our class and said you were missing and wanted to know if anyone had any idea where you might be. So I raised my hand. It was pretty exciting." Mab grinned. "You should have seen Mrs. Hallowell's face when the police turned up!"

"I-I didn't run away. I got in a fight with B-Brandon and his brother last night and I was scared they were going to k-kill King Arthur, so I went back to protect him."

"I didn't think you ran away. That's what I told them." Mab shrugged. "Anyway, it's over. And what's better, now we've got our very own owl. That's so super cool. Don't you think?"

David nodded.

"Want to come over and see him?"

"N-now?"

"Sure, now. Why not? You can come see where we put him, and afterward, if you want, you can stay for dinner. I already asked my mom and she said sure. So, you want to?"

David nodded. "Y-yeah, why not?"

FIFTEEN

David had been to Mab's farm that first night to
help get the incubator, but they'd come up from
the direction of the shed and just gone into one of
the barns. He'd never been around to where the house
was.

Whenever he thought of Mab's farm, he always pictured it like the farms in storybooks, with a big red barn
and a white house with a front porch, but in fact her
house was just an ordinary modern one like people had in
town, and there were about a million barns of all shapes
and sizes and not one of them red. Mab explained that
her father was a dairy farmer, so some of the barns were
for cows giving milk and some were for cows in the winter
and some were for cows having calves and some were for
the calves themselves, after their mothers had gone back
to work being dairy cows. And then there was the hay
shed and the feed shed and the grain shed. It was like a
city of barns.

David didn't see a single one of these cows. He kept a lookout because he'd never been up close to a cow before and was hoping for the chance, but the only animal he saw was an enormous orange tomcat. David called, "Here, kitty, kitty," to it and bent down like he was holding out some cat food because that had always made the Andersons' cats come to him. This one looked at him in a rather disinterested way and sauntered off in the other direction.

David followed Mab through the maze of farm buildings. One low modern barn consisted of nothing but a long line of empty stalls. There was a light but it was only a single bulb hanging in the middle of what was quite a sizable building, so the whole barn was shadowy. Even though the concrete floors were clean, the barn smelled, mostly of cows but also of feed and manure. It wasn't really a stink, but you had to get used to it.

The third stall along from the door was King Arthur's new home. In the stall was a wooden box with straw on the bottom and a heat lamp suspended over it. A piece of wire netting had been fixed over the box in case any barn cats came by.

David bent down to see him. Even all fluffed out, King Arthur was not exactly cute. He was white and fluffy but he still had the monster beak and cartoon feet. His little wings didn't look like wings at all but like arms inside a fuzzy snowsuit.

"C-can I touch him?" David asked.

"You can pat him with a finger, but don't pick him up."

David petted King Arthur's head. It made the little bird's mouth open wide. "L-look, he wants something to eat."

"Yeah, we're going to have to start catching mice soon," Mab said. "He'll be okay for today because baby birds are still absorbing the yolk sac in the first twenty-four hours, but he'll need something tomorrow. So after dinner, we'd better go set some traps."

David had never been to dinner at someone's house before, not as an invited guest. Mab's mother got sort of gushy about how nice it was to meet him and how she'd heard so much about their egg-raising activities from Mab. Only she never once said "Mab." She always said "Madeleine" or "Maddy."

Mab introduced her two brothers. Up until that moment David hadn't even known she'd had brothers, but she did. They were twins, aged two, named Joey and Billy. They looked so alike that David never did figure out which was which.

When dinner was on the table, Mab's father came in. He washed his hands in the sink, and this made Mab's mother tell him off. He laughed heartily and came to the table. He wasn't a very tall man, but David could tell by his muscles he was strong. He had laughing eyes and a mostly bald head with just a bit of hair by his ears. This stuck out in all directions when he took his cap off. He still smelled a bit like cows.

They ate hamburger that had been crumbled up and

cooked in gravy and served with mashed potatoes. David had never had hamburger this way before; so when he saw it, he was worried in case it tasted horrible, because the truth was, it looked pretty strange. But it tasted delicious and he had two helpings. He also ate all his peas, even though he thought peas were sort of nasty, because he'd learned long before that adults could be freaky about vegetables. He just counted himself lucky it was peas and not a vegetable that made the Very Worst Things list, like brussels sprouts. Afterward there was peach pie for dessert.

"So tell me about your egg," Mab's dad said. "Maddy informs me you're the one who found it."

Oh dear. *That* question. David hated being reminded of just how he happened to come into possession of the egg. He prayed Mab's dad would be satisfied with a yes and David wouldn't have to lie. David thought he'd better take action just in case, so he changed the subject.

"I-I'm going to train him."

"We're going to make a hunting owl out of him," Mab added. "Like they did in medieval times. Remember? Like I was telling you about the other day, Dad, about how they had falconers who trained birds to go after rabbits. That's how we're going to train him. I looked it up on the Internet and found a whole bunch of stuff."

"Madeleine, don't talk over your guests," her father said. "I wanted to hear what David had to say."

What David had to say. He liked that. David didn't really have anything to say now, because Mab had just said it all, but he smiled at Mr. Stopes and gave a little nod to show he agreed.

"I think you've done remarkably well to get the bird this far," her dad said. "Not many kids would have the dedication to do that. I must admit, when I heard, I didn't think you'd manage. Owls are hard to rear in captivity. You've clearly got a special talent, David."

David ducked his head but he couldn't keep from grinning.

David felt great when he went home that night. This surprised him, because in the morning he had felt so unhappy. What an amazing day!

The problem with life, however, is that just when you get one part fixed, another part breaks. It took only about two minutes at school the next morning to prove that.

Brandon was leaning against the lockers when David came in. He made a dirty gesture with his hand. David concentrated on doing the combination of his locker.

Then Rodney appeared. He sidled closer and leaned over David's shoulder, like he was trying to see into David's locker. "Hi, Davy, glad to see you found your way to school today."

Brandon joined him. "Yeah, hi, Davy."

"I think Dave here ought to do stuff with us today, don't you?" Rodney said to Brandon. "Because Davy got lost yesterday, didn't he, poor little boy. He had to have a nice policeman come find him. So I think you and me ought to take care of Davy today, so he doesn't get lost again. You come with us, Davy."

The boys didn't give him a chance to say no. Rodney put his arm around David's shoulder on one side and Brandon put his arm around David's shoulder on the other and they squeezed together so tightly that David's arms were pinned to his sides, his hands behind, so that he couldn't jerk away. Then they started marching down the hall.

"We're going to play kickball," Rodney said loudly when they passed Mrs. Hallowell going to her room.

David knew this wasn't going to happen. For one thing, he was the world's worst kickball player because he always missed the ball. No one would *choose* to play kickball with him.

Rodney and Brandon didn't go anywhere near a game. They just walked around the playground with David squished between them, as if they were all the best of friends.

David wanted to stop them, but there was no way to break free without fighting them and he knew if he did, then they'd say he'd started it. After the narrow escape the day before, he didn't dare get into trouble again.

Around and around and around the playground they went. At one point Rodney and Brandon walked right up to the principal who was standing by the swings. "Hello, Mr. Dawson," Rodney said in a very friendly voice.

"Hello, Mr. Dawson," Brandon chimed.

"You boys look like you're having a good time," he replied.

"Yeah, we are!" Rodney said in this cheesy, cheery voice. "David's best friends with me and Brandon now. Huh, David? Aren't you?"

David didn't say anything but he pleaded with his eyes. How could Mr. Dawson believe such garbage? Didn't he *know*?

Off they went again around the playground. "You should have said hello to Mr. Dawson," Rodney said. "He'll think you're stuck up."

Then Rodney's head turned. "Oh *look*!" he said in this really exaggerated way. "*There's* Madeleine Stopes. Let's go say hello to *her*."

David's heart sank.

Madeleine was playing a game with her ball against the side of the school building. When they got over there, quick as a striking snake, Rodney let go of David and grabbed Mab's ball.

"Hey!" she shouted angrily.

"It's mine now," Rodney said, and threw it in the air. "Come on, you guys, let's go play ball."

Brandon let go of David and reached up to catch the ball when Rodney threw it.

"Give me that!" Mab yelled. She chased after Rodney and then, when he threw it, Brandon.

Brandon threw it back to Rodney, and it was clear Mab wasn't going to be able to get it away from them.

David just stood. He wanted to run away really. He wanted to just forget all this was happening, because what *could* he do? He was hopeless at catching balls. Even if he could run like Superman to whisk it away, he'd probably miss catching it. Or drop it. Or trip over his own feet. If he tried to force them to give it back, there'd be a fight and he just couldn't risk a fight right now. He had no idea how to stop them. So he just stood there and did nothing.

Mab started to cry. "Give it to me, you guys. I'm going to tell."

"Bawl-baby," Rodney said. "Why don't you go back to the first grade where you belong?" He made whimpering noises at her but kept tossing the ball back and forth with Brandon.

David desperately wanted to stand up to them. His mouth had gone dry and nasty tasting, so he couldn't get any words out whatsoever. He *wanted* to help, but wanting wasn't enough to make it happen.

Then the bell to go in rang.

"Here, crybaby, here's your stupid ball," Rodney said, but he didn't give it to Mab. Instead, he threw it hard as he could. It went over the playground fence and into the street.

All the other kids were charging for the doors, but David hung back. Mab was already heading for the playground gates to go get her ball. He thought he might go help her, but just then Mr. Dawson came by.

"Come on, David. Time to go in." He put a hand on David's shoulder and pushed him in the right direction. So David had to go in.

SIXTEEN

Mab was really mad at him. David didn't blame her any. He was angry with himself. He should have done something to stop Rodney and Brandon from picking on her. Why hadn't he at least said something? What was the matter with him?

There was no way to avoid going to the farm that afternoon after school because they had to give King Arthur his first meal of dead mouse. Besides, David didn't want to miss out on seeing King Arthur.

He took the long way out to the farm, walking over the fields instead of along the road, because he didn't want the school bus to pass him. Once he got to the farmyard, he got confused by all the barns and it took him a while to find the right one. By the time he got to the stall, Mab was already there. She had a mousetrap with a very dead mouse in it on the floor next to her. Its eyes were all popped out, like two little black beads lying on top of its head.

David let himself into the stall. "H-how is he?"

"Hungry."

David lifted the netting up from the brooding box. King Arthur opened his mouth wide at the sound of the netting going up.

"Here. I brought a knife," Mab said. She had a flat tone to her voice. "We need to cut the mouse up into little bits." She held the knife out to David.

He wanted to point out that "we" meant that she had to help too, not that he had to cut up some gruesome dead mouse all by himself, but he didn't say that. He took the knife.

David had no idea where to start. For one thing, this was a serious sort of knife with a very sharp blade. No one had ever let him handle a knife like this before, and while it was sort of exciting, it was also a little worrying. For a second thing, he had never cut up anything dead before.

Mab watched him. David waited a long moment, trying to get the courage to touch the dead mouse.

"You should have stood up for me," she said at last. Her tone was very low. "You shouldn't have been hanging around with Rodney and Brandon anyway."

"I-I wasn't 'hanging around' with them. They made me."

"Made you what? Be mean to me?"

"I-it wasn't me. I-I didn't join in."

"Yeah, but you were still there. You stood there and let them pick on me. You're supposed to be my friend. You should have defended me."

"I-I wanted to."

"Yes, but you *didn't*. And that's what counts."

David put the knife down and stood up.

"And now you're going to run away," Mab said in a really nasty voice.

He *wasn't* going to run away. That hadn't been his intention at all. It was just that he could feel that prickly feeling in the back of his eyes and he was afraid he was going to cry, and that was the last thing he wanted.

"Yeah, well, if you run away, then King Arthur's mine. Because you're not responsible enough. You're just going to go off and not feed him because you're mad at me."

"I-I'm *not* mad at you!" David said, and he couldn't keep himself from crying. That was so embarrassing that then he *did* want to run away. He went over into the corner of the stall because he didn't want Mab to see him, but he didn't leave. He wasn't about to let Mab have King Arthur.

Mab let out a long, noisy breath behind him.

Keeping his back to her, David wiped his eyes. What was wrong with him, if an eight-year-old girl could make him cry?

Another sigh from Mab. "I just wanted you to stand up for me," she said in a soft voice. "I'm sick of everybody picking on me all the time. I just wanted you to be a friend."

"I-I wanted to stand up for you," David said. "I-I just didn't know what to do. I was scared of g-getting into trouble again." There was other junk he wanted to say, but it melted away into nothingness, leaving him wordless. He turned around, but he couldn't make himself look at her. "I-I'm sorry. Really."

Mab gave sort of a nod. She let out another long breath and then shrugged.

"I-I really, really am."

"Yeah. Okay."

Going back to the knife, David picked it up. Kneeling down on the concrete floor of the stall, he took the mouse and cut it in half. He cut each half in half again. It was gross but he hoped by showing her he was willing to do it, it might make up for things a little.

"I think you're going to have to cut those pieces a lot smaller," Mab said. "And maybe moosh it up some, like it's been chewed. Otherwise it'll be too hard for him to swallow."

Oh *yuck*. David gritted his teeth and cut the mouse down into dinky little grisly pieces.

Very gingerly Mab picked up the piece of mouse that had the tail on it. Holding it by the tail, she lifted the netting on the brooding box. King Arthur opened his mouth wide and Mab just dropped it in. At first King Arthur looked like he was going to choke over it. He kept sticking his neck out and making swallowing movements. Finally it all went down except for the tail. That hung out of King Arthur's mouth. It would have looked funny, if it hadn't looked so gross. A last gulp and that too disappeared.

Mab came back over and picked up another bit of

mooshed, cut-up mouse. Pausing, she looked up at David. "I'm sorry I made you so upset."

"Th-that's okay."

"I didn't really mean it about King Arthur. I was just mad, that's all. We'll still share him."

She held the bit of mouse over King Arthur's head.

"Mab?"

"Yeah?"

"D-do you think we're f-freaks?"

"I dunno. And I don't care, either," she replied. "I don't want to be like other kids just to be like them. They're only interested in boring, stupid stuff most of the time. So I don't want to be like them."

David looked over. "N-never?"

Mab didn't answer.

"I-I do. Sometimes. Sometimes I wish I-I was just like everybody else. I'd like to fit in."

Mab didn't look at him. "I wish people wouldn't call me Teacher's Pet," she said quietly. "Because, know what? I bet I hate Mrs. Hallowell more than anyone else. She's awful to me. If I get something done fast, she says, 'Here, Madeleine, here's some more work *just for you.*' As if because I finished what I was supposed to that means, 'Wow! I like this workbook so well, I want another!' As if. So then the next time I work slower and she comes up to my desk and says, 'Well, I hope this work's not too *hard* for you,' in a voice that really lets me know she really thinks I ought to be back in third grade. And I know she does think that, because she said it to my mom once when

I was there. 'I don't know if Madeleine is socially ready for the fifth grade yet, because she isn't making any friends.' Right in front of me, like I didn't have any ears. So, I'm not her pet." Mab sniggered. "More like I'm her pet peeve!"

"Y-yeah, I wish people would quit saying I'm retarded. I-I wish they'd stop thinking that just because I c-can't talk fast, I can't think."

"Yeah."

"Y-yeah."

"You're *not* retarded, you know," she said, looking over at him. "Nobody who was really retarded would be interested in stuff like you are. Like King Arthur. Or like *King Arthur*." She pointed at the owl and laughed.

"Well, you *can* make friends," David replied. "B-because here's me."

"We're just different, that's all. That's all a freak is. Someone who's different."

David picked up a piece of dead mouse and held it out to King Arthur. "Y-yeah."

"Yeah."

SEVENTEEN

King Arthur did well on his diet of mooshed-up dead things. Mostly it was dead mice, although sometimes Marmalade the cat provided a little variety by catching birds. A couple of times Mab's mother gave them some raw hamburger.

King Arthur grew quickly. By the time he was two weeks old, he was bumping his head against the netting over the brooding box. He was still covered in soft white down, but there were bits of beige feather starting to show underneath. His feet were still enormous compared to the rest of him, and they had grown long, nasty claws. When David mentioned this, Mab pointed out that claws were something cats had. Owls had talons. David said he wasn't looking for the correct name; he was actually meaning how sharp they were. He had scratches everywhere.

After he had been fed, King Arthur would stand up very tall and look over the edge of the brooding box. He would clack his beak together and move back and forth from foot to foot. David loved watching him do this, because he looked like a clumsy dancer just learning steps.

King Arthur didn't like being picked up. He would hunch down when he saw David coming and spread his stubby wings out when David reached in. Sometimes he even hissed. David picked him up anyway, because if King Arthur was going to be a hunting owl, he'd have to get used to being handled. David tried to get him to sit on his shoulder, but King Arthur didn't like this much either. Usually he edged sideways until he tumbled off David's shoulder. If he did stay, he took the opportunity to pull David's hair with his beak or tweak his ear.

One afternoon when King Arthur was three weeks old, Mab's dad came into the barn. He leaned over the stall door and said, "He isn't going to fit in that box much longer."

"Yeah, I know it," Mab replied. "Could you fix some wire up over the stall so that we can leave the netting off?"

"You don't need wire," Mr. Stopes said. "He isn't going to fly for a while yet."

"I'm thinking of the cats," Mab said. "They might get him."

David had King Arthur on his knee. Mab's dad stood for a long moment, watching as David stroked the owl's down. Then he said, "You do know, kids, don't you, that you're not going to be able to keep him forever."

"Why's that?" Mab asked, her brow furrowing.

"He's a wild animal. He isn't meant to be a pet."

"They kept owls in the Middle Ages," Mab said. "Hunting owls."

"They did lots of things differently in those days. Nowadays we know it isn't good for wild animals to be kept in captivity like this," Mr. Stopes replied.

"B-but we're taking good care of him," David said.

"Yes, you are, and I think the two of you need to be commended for that. I'm just saying that when he's old enough, the right thing to do will be to return him to the wild."

"H-he wouldn't live. He's used to us taking care of him."

"No, you couldn't just turn him loose," Mr. Stopes said, "but there are special people who teach animals how to live free again after they've been in captivity."

There was an uncomfortable pause.

"I'm just saying that would be best for King Arthur," Mr. Stopes said.

After he'd gone, David looked over at Mab. "W-we're not really going to let K-King Arthur go, are we?"

"Nah. My dad's just saying that. When he sees how well we train him, he'll change his mind."

At school David still found it hard to hang out with Mab. He didn't feel embarrassed any longer about being friends with her because she was younger or because she was different, but there was this awful thing about *boyfriends* and *girlfriends*. He often imagined what it would be like to go out with some of the girls he saw on

TV or dancing in music videos, but he didn't put Mab into the same category as those girls. But everyone else did. So, to avoid complications, they really didn't hang out a lot together at school.

There was this other kid named Dennis who sat at the table adjacent to David's. He was a quiet kid and most of the time he just blended in so that you didn't realize he was there. He had sparrow-brown hair cut in an ordinary style and his clothes and his shoes came from Sears and not from designer places. He wasn't one of the smart kids who got all A's, but he wasn't one of the ones who needed extra help, either. He was sort of in the middle of everything.

Dennis never had many people hanging around him because he was so quiet. David noticed this and started standing near Dennis during recess and looking available. Unfortunately, even though he was usually never doing anything except standing around, Dennis still never spoke to David. At first David thought maybe he was stuck up and didn't want to talk to him, but then he got to thinking maybe Dennis was just too quiet to start a conversation.

Then one day during science, David noticed Dennis had polar bears for his topic. When they were out at recess and David was standing around, he said, "I-I have an article about polar bears in the book on my table."

Dennis looked at him. For a moment David wished he'd kept quiet, because Dennis really gave him this look, like maybe he had two heads or something.

"I-I-I thought maybe you might want to use it," David added, because he didn't know what else to say.

Dennis smiled very slightly. "Okay."

There was a long pause.

"What are you doing your report on?" Dennis asked.

"P-penguins."

And that's how they started being friends. Dennis began to sit with David at lunchtime. He often went with David when they had to have partners for things in class. They hung out together on the playground. It wasn't that electric kind of exciting being with Dennis, the way it was being with Mab, mainly because Dennis was so hard to talk to. He never said anything, if you didn't ask him. But he seemed to like being asked. And he never made David feel hurried when he couldn't get his own words out. But the best thing about Dennis to David's mind was that he had tried to make a friend and it had worked. Pretty cool.

EIGHTEEN

On the following Saturday afternoon, David was on his way to see King Arthur when a car turned onto his street, a red-and-white Chevy out of the Stone Age, its horn honking.

"David! David!" someone called.

In the passenger seat sat Lily.

David stopped dead in his tracks.

The car stopped and the door opened. "Hey, David!" Lily cried and leaped out. "Cripes, look at you. You never do grow, do you? I thought you'd be taller by now." She hugged him tightly. David hugged back.

Lily looked like the same old Lily with her mass of curly hair and her flat features. Still, she seemed different to David. More like someone he remembered but didn't know. He hadn't seen her since last October, and that felt like forever ago now.

"Wh–what are you doing here?" he asked.

A guy got out of the driver's side of the car. And he *was*

a guy, not a kid. He must have been about twenty-five. He was an unhealthy kind of skinny and had long, greasy black hair. There was a tattoo of a smoking gun on his arm. "That's Mack," Lily said. "He's my boyfriend. Remember? The one I was telling you about."

Mack didn't come around to the sidewalk. Instead, he remained standing by the open door of the car. "Hey, Lily, get him and get in," he said.

Lily said, "Come on."

David shook his head.

"It's just *me*, silly. I came all this way to see you. What are you shaking your head for? Come on. We'll go to McDonald's. I'll buy you something."

"O-okay," David said uncertainly. He got into the back-seat of the car while Lily got in beside Mack.

For once Lily did as she promised and bought David a milkshake. She got herself a diet Coke and asked Mack if there was anything he wanted. The way it seemed to David, Mack was angry. Or maybe just bored. Whatever, he said in a sneery voice that he wanted a beer. Lily seemed to think this was quite a joke, judging from the way she laughed. They went out to sit in the car.

"D-did you run away?" David asked Lily.

Lily didn't answer. Instead, she turned to Mack and said, "You got to excuse him. He's got a brain problem."

"Brainless, eh?" Mack replied. "Now I know he *is* your brother." And he laughed. Even though it sounded like an insult to David, Lily acted like it was hysterically funny. She practically strangled herself on the seat belt, she was falling about laughing so hard.

"Why are you h-here?" David asked.

"Is that the kind of welcome I get?" Lily replied. "Whatever happened to, 'Wow, I'm glad to see you, Lily,' 'Gee, I'm glad you made the effort to come here.' Hey?"

David didn't say anything else. Not that he wasn't glad to see her. He was. Sort of. But *surprised* and *confused* were feelings he felt more.

Lily opened her purse and took out a small notebook. Flipping through the pages to the one she wanted, she handed it over the back seat to David. "See that? That's Mom's address. Where she's living right this minute. I found it on the Internet. I thought we could go see her."

Stunned, David stared at the paper.

"I wrote her a letter," Lily said, "but I think those geezers at the home didn't mail it because I never heard back. She'd write *something*. I know she's probably been wondering all this time about what's happened to us. Probably been looking for us too. So me and Mack decided we're going to go see her, and I said we got to come by here first. I mean, you *are* my baby brother." She grinned over the seat back at him.

How was Lily planning to do this? Just drive up and say, "Hello, remember us? We're your kids"? What did Lily plan to do next? Stay with their mother? What about the children's home? What about Mrs. Mellor? The thing about Lily was that she was always thinking up crazy plans. Once Mrs. Mellor told David that this was part of Lily's problems, but David had never needed anyone to tell him that. He was used to the way Lily thought the wildest ideas could come true. And how they never did.

"Wh-what if it's not Mom?" David ventured.

"It *is*," Lily replied, "because I asked Mrs. Mellor and she said yes, it was her address."

Wow. Walled up in some dungeon-dark part of his mind were David's thoughts about his mother, and he didn't even know really how to get to them. He'd stopped asking questions long ago about where she was or why she had never sent letters or presents or even a card after they were taken away, because not knowing was less scary than most of the reasons David could imagine. He'd gotten used to thinking he didn't really have a mom, that mothers, like dragons or magic spells, belonged only in fairy tales. Now, suddenly, here was Lily saying she knew where their mother was and she was on her way to see her.

He finished his milkshake in silence.

Mack started the car and drove out of the McDonald's parking lot.

"Th-this isn't the right way," David said when he realized Mack was heading for the highway. "My house is back down that other street."

"You're coming with us, aren't you?" Lily asked. She turned around in the front seat and looked at him. "You want to see Mom too, don't you?"

He did. There was no denying that. Even if she couldn't take them back, David wanted to look her in the face. Just so he'd *know* her face, if nothing else.

"We got to stick together, you and me," Lily said. "Blood's thicker than water."

"Would you turn around?" Mack said irritably to Lily. "You're annoying me, hanging over the seat back like that."

"He's my brother, Mack. I haven't seen him in, like, nine months. And him and me, we're all each other's got."

David tried to imagine what meeting his mother would be like.

"Turn *around*," Mack said.

Lily smiled sweetly at him and reached a hand over to caress Mack's cheek, but he jerked away.

Before David realized what was happening, Mack reached out and slapped Lily. Lily whipped around in her seat and faced forward.

In that split-second sound of smacking skin, David did remember his mother. It was as if a kaleidoscope had turned in his head, all the little shards of memory suddenly falling into a new picture. He remembered her grabbing Lily, pulling Lily to the side, raising her hand—

"Stop!" David spoke so loudly Mack slammed on the brakes. "Let me out."

"Christ almighty, kid, I could have had an accident!" Mack cried.

"S-stop the car. I don't want to go."

"Of course you want to go," Lily said, turning around again. The handprint was visible on her cheek. There was a pathetic tone to her voice, like she might cry if he said no.

"I-I want to stay here, Lily."

"In a foster home? You don't want to stay in a foster home, David. You never belong to anyone in a foster home. They just keep passing you around."

"But I-I don't even know Mom, Lily. So I don't want to go see her. If she wanted us, she would have f-found us herself."

"She couldn't, stupid, because she was in jail," Lily replied.

"L-let me out. Stop the car."

"Shut up, kid," Mack said.

David opened the back door. They had already turned onto the highway, so they were going fast. David wasn't going to jump. In fact, he still had his seat belt on, but he hoped this would make Mack stop the car. And it did. He jammed on the brakes so hard that they were all thrown forward. Then he pulled the car roughly over onto the shoulder of the road.

"Get out," he said.

"David, don't," Lily pleaded.

"I-I'm sorry, Lily. I really am. But I want to stay here." And with that, he shut the door.

Mack gunned the engine and the car roared away, spinning gravel in its wake.

David turned and started trudging back toward town. He never looked over his shoulder once.

NINETEEN

With King Arthur growing so fast, Mab and David didn't have time for the King Arthur book anymore. Even though Mab's mother had phoned the school and asked if David could ride to the farm with Mab on the school bus, he wasn't allowed to because the school thought they might get sued if they let extra kids go on the bus and there was an accident. By the time he had walked out to the farm, which was farther than the shed had been, and he and Mab had gone around and found all the mousetraps, emptied the mice out, set the traps again, and fed King Arthur, it was time to start home.

On the weekends, when there was extra time, David would go to the farmhouse and sit at the big kitchen table with Mab and eat cookies and drink milk. He loved drinking milk at the farm. Mab's dad would bring it inside in a big galvanized can from the dairy and tell David it had come straight from the cow. Often it was still warm. At first David thought this sounded seriously yucky and wouldn't taste it, but Mab and her brothers always gave themselves huge milk mustaches and fell about laughing. David didn't want to be left out, so he tried it. It tasted lovely and creamy and not at all like the milk that came out of cartons. Indeed, he now drank so much milk when he was at the farm that Mab's mother was always joking about putting a sign around one of the cows' necks that said, "David's cow."

He had a chance to play with Mab's brothers, too. Mab didn't have much patience with them, but David never minded when they fell in the mud or wet their pants. He liked taking them out to the barns to climb on the hay or feed handfuls of pellets to the calves. Eventually he even learned to tell them apart.

The rest of the time he and Mab just talked.

"I-I want to ask you something."

"What's that?"

"How come your f-folks never call you Mab?"

"They do."

They were emptying mousetraps. She pulled back the spring on one to release the dead mouse into the super-market carrier bag that David was holding.

"Your mother always says Maddy. Your dad usually calls you Madeleine. I'm the only one who ever calls you Mab."

"Lots of people call me Mab. You just haven't heard them."

They were in the hay barn, so David clambered up onto one of the huge round bales. He sat astride it like a horse.

Mab stayed down below and reset the trap.

"Know what I-I think? I think you just *w-want* that name, but no one really calls you that. Except me," David said.

"No sir."

"Y-yes sir."

"You don't know everyone who talks to me." Her voice was edgy.

David didn't want to make her mad, so he said, "It d-doesn't matter. I don't care."

Mab started to climb up on the bales from the other side.

"I-I like Mab. It fits you."

She nodded. "I'm going to make it my real name when I grow up. You can do that—change your name for real. Then everyone *has* to call you that."

"R-really?"

"It costs money. I don't know how much. But I'm going to do it because I hate Madeleine. Madeleine sounds like someone who ought to live in a city and spend all her time shopping for expensive shoes."

David missed the King Arthur stories.

"Would you m-mind," he asked Mab one afternoon, "if I borrowed the King Arthur book?"

Mab didn't mind at all. She took him up to her room. She was right in saying it wasn't as big as his room, but he would have traded her any day. For one thing, she had her own computer. For another, she had about a million books and they were all hers. David didn't have a single book that was really his.

When David got home that night, Granny was just taking macaroni and cheese, all crusty and brown on top, out of the oven. "Look," she said, "I've made your favorite."

"Look," he said back, "I-I've got the King Arthur book. Mab lent it to me."

David sat down at the table and showed Granny the pictures. "There's Sir Gawain. And that's K-King Arthur. And Queen Guinevere. And there—" David pointed. "There's Excalibur."

Granny examined the fine, feathery drawings. "What an old book this is," she said. "This book was already old when I was a little girl."

"T-tonight, later, would you read it to me?" David asked.

Granny smiled. "Yes, of course."

David smiled. He felt good. Like he was rich. Even though he was poor compared to most kids, compared to Mab with all her books and her computer. But just then with the macaroni and cheese on the table and the King Arthur book sitting beside him and Granny saying she'd read it, David felt like he was rich.

One afternoon David fed King Arthur alone because Mab was at the orthodontist. He walked through the barns, looking for mousetraps. Coming into the big cow barn, he ran into Mab's dad.

"David, just the person I was looking for." Mr. Stopes had a small box in his hand. "I have a present for you."

When David pulled the top off, his excitement turned to yuck, because there were three dead chicks inside. He tried hard to hide his disappointment. And his embarrassment that he'd believed there really was a present.

"I thought you could give them to King Arthur," Mr. Stopes said. "It'll give him a little variety in his diet."

"Th-thank you," David said and peered at the dead chicks. He was thinking icky thoughts about cutting them up.

"You know, I've been very impressed by the way you and Mab have cared for this little owlet. You show a lot of responsibility for your age."

David looked up.

"Not many children would be so reliable. I'll bet your family is very proud of you."

"I-I don't have a family," David said. "Except my sister, but she doesn't live with me."

"What about Granny?"

"She's my f-foster mother, not my real f-family."

"People don't have to be related to you to be your family. Family comes from caring for each other," Mr. Stopes said. "And caring about each other. And I expect Granny is very proud of what a responsible young man you are. How old are you?"

"I-I'll be twelve in May."

"Because what I'm thinking, David, is that maybe you'd like a job. To earn some money."

123

David grinned and went to nod when suddenly a horrible thought struck him. Just a few days earlier, Mrs. Hallowell had asked him how in the world he ever expected to get a job in life if he didn't learn to read better?

"What's the matter?" Mr. Stopes asked. "Suddenly you look unhappy."

David didn't know what to say.

"Don't you like the idea? Because if you don't want to, that's okay. It won't upset me."

"N-no, I do like the idea. It's just . . ." David sucked in a long breath. "M-maybe Mab's told you . . . about why I'm older. I-I got held back in school. I-I can't do work very well."

"That's one kind of work. But it doesn't mean you can't do another kind of work. In fact, maybe it means the farm is just the right place for you. Seeing you with your owl and how dedicated you've been to caring for him, I'm thinking you're the kind of boy who belongs on a farm. You're smart with animals."

David smiled.

"And I certainly could use a hard-working, responsible person for a couple of hours on Saturday afternoons."

"A real j-job? Yes, I do want to. I-I'll ask Granny tonight. I'll phone later and let you know, okay?" And with that David picked up the box of dead chicks and zoomed off, because if he'd stayed any longer, his face would probably have cracked open, he was smiling that hard.

TWENTY

David went out to the farm at two o'clock on Saturdays and worked until five. Mostly he worked in the shed where the calves were. He learned to mix up their milky feed and pour it into the tubs. One calf was sick, so he had to put its milk into a big plastic Coke bottle with a huge nipple on it and give it to the calf like you did with a baby. At first the calf refused to suck from the bottle, so Mr. Stopes showed David how to stick his fingers into the calf's mouth to encourage him, After feeding the calves, David had to clean out the dirty straw and put down clean bedding. This was a stinky job but it made the calves playful, and he loved having them bounce around him.

Other times he went out on the tractor with Mr. Stopes. Mostly they drove along the fences, looking for places that needed to be fixed, although once they went up into the broad field where Mr. Stopes made hay in the summer. When they were up there, he let David steer the tractor and told him that when he was taller, he'd teach him how to drive it.

Granny made him open a bank account and put half of his weekly earnings in savings, but David got to keep the other half. He saved it in a jar in his underwear drawer until he had enough to buy a radio. It was small and not very fancy, but now when he was in bed, he could listen to whatever he wanted, whenever he wanted, and no one could tell him to stop wasting the batteries or change to a better station.

By the first week in May, King Arthur was five weeks old. He had almost reached his adult size and he had most of his proper feathers in place underneath the white down. They grew from the same quills as the down, pushing the down out so that it stuck all tufty at the ends of the new adult feathers. This gave King Arthur a dishevelled look, as if a pillow had exploded over him.

He no longer needed the brooding box, although he still enjoyed sitting in it. Mab's dad had put wire around the stall, turning it into a super-sized cage, and one Saturday David helped him put a perch up along the back.

Whenever David and Mab arrived, King Arthur got excited because he knew they meant food. He loved a good meal. Anticipating his tasty cut-up mice, he would clack his bill together while they prepared his food, and then he'd clack it for several minutes after he was done eating, as if he were saying how good it was.

Once he'd eaten, King Arthur was always wide awake and

interested in action. His wings weren't yet strong enough to bear his weight, so he liked David to lift him up to his perch. He could get back down again by sort of throwing himself at the brooding box. From the height of his perch, King Arthur stretched his neck out and swivelled his head to see over into the other stalls. If he saw something interesting, he bobbed up and down fast. If it was really something good, he stretched his wings out, as if he were going to fly, and occasionally flapped them up and down, but if he got too excited doing this, he fell right off the perch!

Although he couldn't fly yet, King Arthur was quite capable of hopping out of his box anytime he wanted. This landed him on the stall floor and there he found all sorts of things to "hunt," like small clumps of dirt or leaves. His favorite prey, though, was straw. He'd spot a piece, stare at it hard, then hop along the floor in silly little skips, like a girl playing "Mother May I." Then *pounce!* Once he landed on the straw, he spent ages trying to pick it up with his foot and transfer it to his mouth. Once he had accomplished that, he never seemed to know what to do with it next, so he just held it and looked around, but David always thought he looked pleased with himself.

"We ought to start teaching him to hunt for real," Mab said one afternoon. She pulled a long piece of string from her pocket. "I'm going to tie this to a mouse tail and drag it around for him."

David lifted King Arthur out of his box. He had to be careful doing this because King Arthur's talons were really sharp now and could cut skin easily so he had to wear a sturdy work glove. David had to be careful where he put King Arthur too, because King Arthur pooped a lot. It looked like white tempera paint and went everywhere. Granny had gotten mad more than once about the state of his clothes.

Mab dragged the mouse around. King Arthur was sitting on David's shoulder and didn't take any notice. He was more interested in pulling David's hair.

Mab tried again.

"He d-doesn't want to do it," David said. "He's too f-full. Maybe tomorrow, before we feed him."

Mab regarded King Arthur for several moments. "Do you think we should turn him loose when he gets older?" she asked, her voice thoughtful.

"*No.*"

"My dad says we're going to have to."

David transferred King Arthur to his perch. "We're going to tr-train him, so we can't let him go."

"I know that's what we planned to do," she said slowly, "but my dad keeps talking to me about it. He says doing that wouldn't make King Arthur happy. He says the right thing to do is set him free."

"H-he's happy. You can tell. L-look how he clacks his beak together. Th-that's his happy sound. And he likes it when you rub the side of his head." David put a finger up and scratched along King Arthur's neck. The feathers were sleek there, because he'd lost almost all the down around his shoulders.

"There's this guy my dad knows," Mab said. "He lives over near Millville and he's a zoology professor. He has a sanctuary where he takes care of wild animals that have been hurt on the road and stuff. After the vet fixes them, he sends them to this guy and cares for them and then teaches them how to go back into the wild."

"*I–I'd* like that job."

"My dad was in Millville yesterday and he met this guy at the feed store. Dad told him about King Arthur, and you know what he said? He said most likely King Arthur is going to die if he stays with us."

"N-no he won't," David said in surprise. "We're taking really good care of him. Even your d-dad said that."

"But this man said we can't give him the right diet. He needs a variety of stuff."

"H-he gets a variety. He got the dead chicks. That r-robin that Marmalade caught the other day. We can't let him go. H-how would we make a hunting owl out of him then?"

Mab sighed. "I know, but . . ." There was a long pause. "I don't want to let him go either. I love him just as much as you do. But when my dad is telling me this stuff . . . well, what if he's right, David? It'd be so awful if something happened to King Arthur just because we thought we were taking great care of him but really we should have been letting him go."

"No," David said firmly. "H-he's going to be a hunting owl. That was the whole p-point of doing this. Anyway, he's my owl. I-I found the egg. So I get final say."

TWENTY-ONE

David's birthday was on the fifth of May. He asked Granny if he could invite Mab for dinner that night. Granny said that was a great idea.

She made David's favorite meat—pot roast—and a humongous chocolate cake. When Mab arrived, her hair was in a ponytail held with a colorful beaded tie, and she had this clean look, like she'd been made to take a bath right beforehand. She was carrying a birthday present wrapped in shiny silver paper.

"You're never going to guess what it is," she said. "It was *really* hard for me to get."

David shook the box. Something thunked heavily against the side. Tearing the paper from it, David lifted the lid off. Inside was the King Arthur book.

"See!" Mab said gleefully. "That's why it was so hard. Because I had to ask your granny to get it for me when you didn't know, so I could wrap it up!"

"I-it's mine?"

"Yeah, I'm giving it to you. I mean, you might as well own it. You have it all the time anyway."

"*Wow!*" David grinned. "Thanks!"

"And here's your other present," Granny said and came though the kitchen doorway. She was wheeling a bike.

"*Wow!*" David cried again, because he'd never had his own bike. The only time he'd been able to ride a bike in the past was if the other kids in the foster families had let him use theirs.

"It isn't new, I'm afraid," Granny said. "It belonged to Mrs. Worthington's son, but he's away at college now and it's got a lot of life left in it. And I thought you could use a bike to save you time getting back and forth to Mab's farm."

David biked out to the farm on Saturday afternoon to do his work for Mr. Stopes, but first he stopped by King Arthur's stall.

The moment David saw him, he could tell the owl wasn't well. Sitting in his box, King Arthur was all fluffed up. His eyes were half shut.

"Wh-what's the matter, boy?" David asked, bending over the box. He rubbed beneath King Arthur's chin. "Do you need to sick up a pellet?" This was one of King Arthur's more disgusting things. At least once a day he had to throw up all the mouse bones and fur and other things he couldn't digest. Usually he just erped it up and didn't look bothered about it, but David wondered if maybe it could make him feel awful first.

David tickled him under his chin again, but King Arthur just sat, fluffed up.

Going over to the farmhouse, David knocked at the back door. "Is M-Mab here?" he asked when Mab's mother came to the door.

"Maddy?" she called. "David's here."

Mab boinged through the kitchen like Tigger and landed with a big bouncy step on the back door.

"K-King Arthur looks sick. Maybe he needs a vet."

Mab came out to the barn to see for herself. David wanted to take him to the vet immediately, but Mab's mother couldn't drive them because the twins were both having their naps. So David and Mab searched for her dad until they found him in the tractor shed and explained how sick King Arthur looked.

The vet had a fancy-looking waiting room with pine paneling halfway up the walls and, above the paneling, wallpaper with blue pawprints all over it. The room smelled like a hospital except there was also sort of a doggy whiff. Three other people were also in the waiting room. One had a plaintively mewing calico cat in a pet carrier. Another had a slobbery black dog with sticky-up ears, and the third had a teeny tiny dog that looked like a furry sofa cushion. This dog barked constantly.

Sitting with the cardboard box on his lap, David could feel King Arthur shifting about inside and making a faint hissy sound because he didn't like the barking dog. David didn't either. It was annoying and he decided right then and there that when he got a dog of his own someday, it definitely wasn't going to be the yappy kind.

When David opened the box, the vet looked surprised. He didn't actually know much about owls, he said. Then he lifted King Arthur out and felt him all over. King Arthur voiced his displeasure at the vet by making clicky little alarm noises.

"He seems very thin," the vet remarked.

"We feed him all the time," Mab said. "And he always eats everything. Except today. He wasn't hungry."

"You do know you aren't supposed to take a bird out of the wild?" the vet said. "Actually, it's against the law."

"W-we didn't take him out of the wild," David replied. "We h-hatched him ourselves."

"I'm afraid that's against the law too. No one is supposed to touch the eggs of birds of prey without a special license."

"M-maybe we could get a license," David suggested. "Does it cost much money?"

"I think a better idea might be to return him to a more natural environment. Odds are, he's ill because he's living in captivity."

David didn't like this vet. First he said he didn't know much about owls, and now he was lecturing on how to take care of them.

"I think what you should do is take him to Dr. Pellam," the vet said. "That'd give your owl the best chance of survival." Dr. Pellam was the zoology professor Mab's dad knew.

133

Once they were out in the car, Mr. Stopes said, "I suppose we could drive over to Millville and see what Daniel Pellam has to say."

Daniel Pellam lived in a cabin in the woods up a very bumpy road about fifteen miles outside Millville. The place was like a zoo. There were pens everywhere with badgers and foxes and other animals. David would have loved to investigate further, if he'd just come to visit, but as it was, he felt nervous and ill at ease.

Dr. Pellam didn't look at all like David had expected a professor to look. He didn't have glasses or wild gray hair or a distracted expression. He was about the same age as Mab's dad and had lots of floppy black hair and the crinkly sort of face you get from being outdoors too much. He was dressed in jeans and a wool plaid shirt like a hunter would wear.

David carried King Arthur's box into the cabin. It wasn't a house at all inside, but a kind of animal hospital. There were more pens, some empty, others with birds in them, mostly things like crows. One had a chipmunk. In the middle of the room was a large wooden table. Dr. Pellam told David to set the box there.

"Ah," Dr. Pellam said when he opened the box, "*Asio flammeus.*" He smiled at Mab and David. "That's his Sunday name."

"His name the rest of the week is K-King Arthur," David said tartly.

"King Arthur, hey?" Dr. Pellam replied cheerfully,

ignoring David's tone. "A lordly name. Are you a King Arthur fan?"

David didn't answer.

"*Asio flammeus* is his formal Latin name. All living things have a Latin name. Humans too. We're *Homo sapiens.*"

Now Mab was miffed. David could tell she thought Dr. Pellam didn't believe they knew anything, so she said, "I thought the Latin genus name was *Bubo.*"

"*Bubo* is the great horned owl. King Arthur is a short-eared owl. He's *Asio.*"

Dr. Pellam lifted King Arthur gently out of the box. King Arthur didn't struggle against him, as he had the vet.

"What have you been feeding him?"

Mab explained about trapping and cutting up the mice.

"Hmmm." Dr. Pellam lifted up one of King Arthur's wings. He felt underneath it. "Has he been making owl pellets?"

Both David and Mab nodded.

"Has he been going to the bathroom?"

"Lots," David said. "H-he goes when he gets excited."

"Other times too, David," Mab added.

"Y-yes, but when he hunts straw, he makes little splats all across the floor as he chases it. Is that normal?"

"Sure is," Dr. Pellam said. "You know, I'm impressed with you two. You obviously both know a lot about owls and you've done remarkably well to get him this far. I can tell you love King Arthur very much."

Pride flowed through David. He grinned over at Mab.

"The problem is, owls are wild birds. And we can't make something tame just by loving it enough. Even though we know a lot, we still don't know enough about wild creatures. So even when we have the best intentions, what we do often hurts more than it helps.

"I think King Arthur may have had too many mice. It's possible he's gotten parasites from the mice. Or perhaps some of the mice he's had have eaten poison put down for rats. When this happens, the poison will build up in King Arthur's body. If he were eating lots of other things as well—small birds, voles, shrews, that sort of thing—it wouldn't matter so much if one of the mice had poison, but it will make him very ill if he'd eaten a lot of them. Owls need a varied diet, just like you and me."

"H-he's had a varied diet," David said. "D-dead chicks. And birds. And stuff killed on the road." Which wasn't true, but David had just thought of doing that to get King Arthur other meat. He was *going* to do it. From now on. From now on he was going to do an even better job of taking care of King Arthur.

Dr. Pellam nodded. "Yes, I can tell you've done your best. But we don't want anything to happen to King Arthur, do we?"

Mab's dad reached out and touched David's shoulder. "I think what Dr. Pellam is saying is that it would be better—"

David jerked away. "I-I *know* what Dr. Pellam is saying!" he retorted, his voice much louder than he'd meant. "And he *can't* have him! H-he's not taking King

Arthur away. King Arthur is *mine*."

"Technically, David," Dr. Pellam said in a quiet voice, "it's against the law. People need a license to handle wild birds."

"Then I'll *get* a stupid license!" David cried.

Mab's dad reached out again and touched his shoulder. "Dan, David is a very talented boy with animals. He works for me on Saturdays and I've seen the things he can do. I'm sure when he's had a chance to think things through, he'll do what's best for King Arthur."

"G-give him back!"

Dr. Pellam and Mr. Stopes exchanged looks and David knew the looks were saying, "He's going to give you King Arthur," and this made David livid. It was just like being with Mrs. Mellor and his foster parents when they'd decided they'd had enough and wanted David to live somewhere else. It was this he's-a-kid-he'll-adjust look. No matter how much he cared, no matter how much he *didn't* want something, they just went ahead and did it and he had no choice but to accept it.

Except this was different. King Arthur *belonged* to him. You didn't give up things that belonged to you as if they didn't matter. You took care of them. So David swiftly lifted King Arthur off the table and put him back in the box.

"Give us a little time to talk it over," Mr. Stopes said to Dr. Pellam. "I'm sure David will do the right thing."

Dr. Pellam nodded. "Perhaps when summer vacation comes, you can visit King Arthur here and I can show you

how I'll teach him to be a wild owl again. Perhaps someday this might even be work you'd be interested in learning how to do."

Ignoring him, David clutched the box to his chest.

The ride home from the wildlife sanctuary was dread-
ful. No one spoke. David kept a tight hold on King
Arthur's box and stared out the window, wishing he and
King Arthur were a million miles away.

Back at the farm, Mab and David took King Arthur to
his stall.

"I know how you feel," Mab ventured at last.

"N-no, you don't," David muttered.

"I love him too. Just as much as you do, so I don't want
to give him up either," she replied. "I feel like crying, just
thinking about it. I understand."

"You *don't*!" David shouted. "You think you do because
you're so smart, but you *don't*. You have everything. A cat.
A computer. A farm. You have brothers and a mom and a
dad. I-I don't even *know* my parents. Even my sister's
gone now. All I've got is King Arthur."

"You've got more than that, David," she said. "You've
got Granny. You've got *me*."

"You don't *belong* to me though."

"What do you think 'belong' means? It means taking
care of each other. It means caring what happens to
someone. Caring so much that you won't let anything bad
happen to them, even when it means you don't get what
you want. And *that's* what I'm saying." She looked up at

him. "*I* don't want to give King Arthur up either, because I love him too. But *because* I love him, it's even more important to me that nothing bad happens to him."

"It's b-because he's not yours. You didn't find his egg. *I-I* did. So you don't understand at all!" David shouted, and stomped out.

David should have stayed to do his farm work but he was too angry. Finding his bike, he started to pedal for home.

Then he stopped. Letting the bike slow down until it came to a halt, David dropped his feet to the ground. Looking back down the drive toward the farm, he realized what he had to do.

TWENTY-TWO

It was already dusk by the time David got home. As he came toward the back door, he could see Granny in the kitchen.

"This is a bad habit of yours," she said when he came in. "Do you know what time it is? Dinner was ready fifteen minutes ago." Her eyebrows pulled together, pushing up squiggles of skin above her nose. "What's in that box?"

"K-King Arthur," David said, and set the box on the table.

"Your owl? Good heavens, don't put it on the table where we're going to eat." She approached the box carefully. The lid was shut tightly, but there were scratching noises coming from inside.

"I-I'm going to keep him here for a while. Mab's dad needed the stall where we were keeping him there."

"Don't they have other stalls? Seems like a farm would be a far better place for an owl than my kitchen," Granny replied.

"We've g-got to give him something different to eat,"

David said, hoping this was a good enough answer to her question. "We took him to the vet today and I'm not supposed to give him any more mice for a while. Th-they've got poison in them. So, do we have any hamburger?"

"Goodness," Granny said, her voice uncertain.

David picked up the box and started for the little staircase behind the door.

"You've got another think coming, if you had plans to keep him in your bedroom," Granny said. "I think the garage would be a better place for owls."

"Awww," David said in a disappointed tone. "Just for a little while? Okay? L-let me put him up there just until after supper."

Granny rolled her eyes. "Well, just until after supper then. And don't you *dare* let him out of that box."

After supper David took some raw hamburger from the refrigerator to feed King Arthur. He opened the lid of the box. King Arthur peered out. He looked like he felt a little better.

Gently David scratched around his neck, because King Arthur particularly liked this. Then he held out the hamburger. King Arthur noted it but didn't open his mouth.

"C-come on. Try this. You'll like it."

King Arthur looked at him.

"C-come on." With his other hand, David stroked under King Arthur's beak because sometimes this made him open his mouth. King Arthur squawked and flapped his wings.

David kept trying until at last King Arthur nibbled a

bit of the hamburger. David offered a little more and he took it. Then he ruffled his feathers and ignored David.

Mab phoned early the next morning. "What *have* you *done?*" she hissed angrily.

"He's better," David said. "He ate hamburger r-really well last night." Which wasn't exactly true, but David knew he had to say something to calm her down.

"I'm going to tell. You had no right to take him."

"He's *b-better*, Mab. Didn't you hear me? I-I want to keep him awhile. Then they'll see we can take good enough care of him."

The other end of the phone went silent.

"Please?" David said. "Just l–let me try."

"I don't think you should," Mab said, but there was hesitation in her voice.

"I think he just needed a ch-change," David said. "He *is* better. He ate for me last night."

He could hear Mab sigh.

Just then David saw Granny coming in from the backyard, where she'd been hanging out the laundry. "Listen, I-I've got to go. Anyway, don't worry about it. Th-this'll work out. And we'll get to keep him."

"Okay," Mab said uncertainly. She hung up.

Sunday was a bit of a disaster. David hadn't been able to take the brooding box, which King Arthur still stayed in at night, because it was too bulky. So he'd moved the owl in the cardboard box they'd used to take him to the vet. Left alone with it, King Arthur took less than an hour to pull the box to shreds.

David had found him a new, sturdier, larger box in the garage the night before. Since he didn't have any straw, he'd put rags in to make a nice bed and then shut the flaps down so that King Arthur couldn't pull that box apart. But King Arthur wasn't used to having a lid shut down over him and David was worried about his having enough air, so in the end David had gone back down again and opened the flats. Then he put an old cake rack over the top of the box to keep King Arthur in.

Unfortunately, King Arthur had had no difficulty dealing with that setup. He'd knocked the rack off, tipped over the box, and spent the night walking all around the garage, hopping up on stuff, knocking other stuff over, and making a huge mess. So the first half of Sunday David spent cleaning the garage. It wasn't until almost lunchtime that David could take King Arthur upstairs.

Granny, of course, was not keen on an owl upstairs, so David had to beg a lot. That he had cleaned the garage up so well helped, and finally Granny gave in when he promised, promised, *promised* to keep King Arthur in his box.

Then it was time for Sunday dinner, which Granny always had at lunchtime. David poked dinky holes along the top rim of the box, too small for King Arthur to get his beak into, and then he put the flaps down on the cardboard box while he went to eat. When he came back, he discovered King Arthur had managed to squeeze through the closed flaps and get out of the box. He had then pulled himself up onto David's bed. So when David entered, there was King Arthur perched on the iron frame at the head of his bed.

"Oh geez! You p-pooped everywhere, King Arthur!"

White splats marched across his floor and decorated his bedspread. Worse, though, there were also lots of white splats all over his pillow. And a great big owl pellet that King Arthur had sicked up. "Oh geez, King Arthur! Oh *yuck*! C-come down from there."

When David climbed onto the bed to get him, King Arthur jumped off the iron bedstead. He couldn't fly yet but he could run very quickly.

David chased after him, but the more he chased, the more King Arthur hurried around the room, knocking stuff over, flapping his ineffective wings, and making alarmed little squawks. And the more he pooped. David groaned. If there was anything he'd learned about owls, it was how messy they were.

At last David managed to throw a dirty shirt over King Arthur's head and catch him. "B-bad owl, look what you've done to my room," he said as he brought King Arthur back to his box. "I'm going to have to change my sheets *and* my spread before Granny finds out. And my pillowcase. And probably my whole stupid p-pillow. Who wants to sleep in a bed with owl poop all over it?" He smoothed King Arthur's feathers and scratched his neck.

"Guess what I've got? Hamburger. Look." David unwrapped the napkin he'd brought upstairs and pinched off a piece.

King Arthur was definitely hungry. Maybe all the fun he'd had wrecking David's room had helped work up an appetite, because he gobbled down the hamburger.

"G-good boy!" David said. He ended up giving King Arthur a big meal. It had been more than two days since he'd eaten much, so David reckoned he was really hungry.

Afterward David set King Arthur on the floor because he thought he'd want to play at hunting like he did in the stall. There wasn't any straw here, of course, so David searched for something similar. The only thing he could find was a pencil. He rolled it enticingly across the floor.

King Arthur didn't try to hunt it. He just sat. But he did seem interested, because he watched it rolling.

After he stripped the messy bedding, David got a green towel out of the bathroom and draped it over the iron rail at the foot of his bed so that King Arthur could sit there without making a big mess.

Then he got out the King Arthur book and sat down on the bed with it. Maybe if he showed his King Arthur *this* King Arthur . . . David smiled to himself. It was a silly idea. He knew owls couldn't focus well up close and he knew King Arthur wouldn't have the faintest idea what he was showing him anyway. In fact, David would have to watch out that King Arthur didn't try and grab the pages and tear them. But he still liked the idea anyway.

TWENTY-THREE

David spent most of Sunday with King Arthur. He had a great time, even with the mess. Mostly he tried to amuse King Arthur with different things to hunt or chase, or he did silly things like getting Excalibur down from the wall and playing at being King Arthur himself, bouncing around on his bed and waving his stick. This was little-kid stuff and David would have been mortified if anyone had seen him playing like that, but it was fun.

King Arthur, the owl, was not all that impressed with David's bouncing around. He clacked his beak and spread out his wings in alarm. When he got really concerned, he puffed up all the feathers along the back of his head, which made him look like he had a Native American headdress on, because he still had tufty little bits of down on the ends of his adult feathers. David couldn't help but laugh at him. Then he felt sorry for having scared him and decided to give him another meal of hamburger to make up for it. King Arthur gulped down the offering willingly. As David fed him, he thought how pleased Mab was going to be when she saw how bright and healthy King Arthur was in David's care. Then she'd know he'd done the right thing in taking him.

David gave King Arthur two more big meals before bedtime, just to build him up. Then it was time to put him back into his cardboard box in the garage.

David didn't want the same thing to happen as the previous night, so he pushed together the two garbage cans that were kept in there, plus some packing boxes, to form a small enclosure.

"T-tomorrow I'll start to make you a real cage," David said as he lowered the cardboard box into the enclosure. He had already gotten his bank book out to see how much money he had. He hadn't asked Granny yet, but he was sure she'd let him use his money to buy materials.

King Arthur was clearly interested in perching. Before David could put the cake rack over the open box, King Arthur had already attempted to get up on the edge. This made it tip over, and the rags on the bottom fell out, startling him.

David leaned into the enclosure and righted the box. He put King Arthur back in. "You d-don't want to do that. You want your box to sleep in. T-tomorrow I'll find you a nice big branch and fix it in here for you to perch on."

Granny called from the kitchen, saying it was getting late.

"I-I got to go," David said to the owl. He patted King

Arthur's head. "See you in the morning." Then he turned off the light and left.

David set his alarm for half an hour earlier, so he'd have enough time to take care of King Arthur before school. First he went to the refrigerator and took out some hamburger to let it warm up to room temperature so that it wouldn't be too cold for King Arthur to eat. Then he got dressed and ate his own breakfast.

As he was opening the door to the garage, David was thinking about what he could find to entertain King Arthur while he was at school. Going to the enclosure, David peered in. King Arthur was lying down in the cardboard box.

"Hey, s-sleepyhead, wake up." David pushed aside one of the garbage cans so that he could get inside the enclosure too. He reached down and nudged King Arthur. "I've got your breakfast."

King Arthur didn't move.

David's throat grew tight, as if someone had a hand around it, strangling him. He pushed the owl again. "W-w-wake up! *Wake* up!"

King Arthur didn't.

Dropping the hamburger, David ran back into the house.

"What's the matter?" Granny asked. She was at the sink.

David was crying too hard to speak, so he just pointed toward the garage.

Granny wiped her hands dry on her apron and followed

David back out. "Oh dear," she said when she looked at the box. "Poor little birdie."

David thundered up to his room and slammed the door. Once there he felt like he *had* to hit something or his body was going to explode like a detonated bomb. He grabbed Excalibur off the wall and swung it at his bed. It snapped in two. He hit the half still in his hands against the iron railing again. It broke again. Then he felt even worse, because now Excalibur was gone too. He was crying so hard he couldn't catch his breath.

Granny came up the stairs, gave a little knock and opened the door. "I phoned the school. I said you wouldn't be coming in today."

"It isn't *fair!*" David cried angrily. "I took such good care of him. I did everything I could. This shouldn't have happened. It isn't fair."

"No," Granny said. "You're right. It isn't fair."

Here, David knew without a doubt, was *the* Very Worst Thing. All those other things, they were just garbage. *This* was the real top of the list. King Arthur was dead. All that effort, all that time, everything he'd dreamed of doing . . . He'd loved King Arthur so much. Now there was nothing.

David cried and cried. Every time he stopped, he'd think about how much he missed King Arthur or how he wasn't going to get to train him or how he wasn't even going to get to see King Arthur fly, and the tears would start all over again.

Then the worse thoughts started. It was his fault King Arthur had died. He should never have wrecked King Arthur's nest to begin with and chased his real mother off. David had always tried very hard not to remember what had happened on that hillside in early March. Now he did think about it, and how King Arthur would probably be alive and free this very minute if he'd left the nest alone.

And it was his fault for not listening to Mab. She was, after all, a girl genius, and he was plain stupid. Everyone knew that. He should have paid attention to her and her dad and let Dr. Pellam keep King Arthur.

He was still lying on his bed when Granny came upstairs again.

She sat down on the edge of his bed. She didn't speak but just reached over and rubbed his back between his shoulder blades.

"I-I feel so horrible," David said. He began to cry again. "Everything's my fault."

"You took good care of him," Granny said softly. "You loved him a lot and you thought you were doing the best for him. But sometimes these things happen, even though we do love something very much. Sometimes the worst happens."

"*Why?*"

"I don't know. Sometimes it's just that way."

"It shouldn't be," David muttered. "It isn't right."

"No," Granny said, her voice very quiet, "but even so, sometimes it still happens that way."

TWENTY-FOUR

In the afternoon David came downstairs and watched TV. It was all boring stuff. Mostly stupid quiz shows or soap operas where everyone had something horrible happen to them, even the people who were the good guys. Or talk shows where everyone had something horrible happening to them for real. David watched anyway.

It kept him from thinking about Mab, because how was he going to tell her this news? Would she ever forgive him for taking King Arthur? Probably he had lost Mab as well as King Arthur.

Granny had gone over to Mrs. Forman's. Mrs. Forman had a gigantic house on Exeter Street and it took a long time to clean, so David knew not to expect her back before four o'clock. He got fed up watching TV and couldn't think of what else to do. He didn't even feel like eating the cookies Granny had left out for him.

Putting on his shoes, David walked out to the garage. Granny had put King Arthur's body into a shoe box and laid it on the workbench. David took the lid off. Reaching in, he touched King Arthur's feathers. He touched the funny downy bits that were sticking to the ends of the adult feathers. Yesterday they were growing, David thought. Now they would never change into adult plumage. Sudden as that.

He petted King Arthur's head and scratched him the way he'd liked to be scratched along the side of his neck. Tears came to David's eyes. Then he fingered King Arthur's talons, feeling how sharp they were. He stretched out one of King Arthur's wings, which King Arthur would never have let him do if he were alive. But everything felt the same—stiff and cold. Dead.

Taking a shovel down from the rack on the wall of the garage, David went out along the flowerbed beside the house where there were tulips blooming. Beside a shrub with tiny pink blossoms that had a strong, sweet smell, there was a bare spot of ground. David dug deep. Then he went inside, upstairs to his room.

He meant to find anything that was soft and warm to wrap King Arthur in, but when he got up there, what he saw first was Little Blanket. He looked at it. It was the only thing that had belonged to him forever, the only thing that had felt comforting through all the changes. David picked it up. Maybe it would be a comfort to King Arthur. Wherever King Arthur had gone, maybe he wouldn't feel so lonely if he had Little Blanket with him. It would smell like David, so maybe he would feel David was still with him.

Taking Little Blanket down to the garage, David kissed King Arthur's head and then gently wrapped him up in it. He placed him in the shoe box and closed the lid. Going outside with it, David laid the shoe box carefully in the hole. Then he took the spade and covered it up.

"Good-bye, King Arthur," he said, and that made him cry again.

When Granny came home, she started to make macaroni and cheese for supper. That good, cheesy smell floated up the little staircase and into David's room as he lay on his bed.

David didn't want anything to eat. Instead he lay on his bed, thinking about the Very Worst Things list and putting it in order.

"David?" Granny called. "Time for supper."

David just lay.

Granny's footsteps came quietly up the stairs. When she came into the room, David rolled away from her and faced the wall.

"Don't you want supper? It's macaroni and cheese."

"I-I'm not hungry."

Granny sat down on the bed. "I know how you feel."

David reckoned there ought to be a law against people saying they knew how you felt.

"Shall I tell you a story?" Granny asked, but she didn't wait for him to answer. "It's not a story I tell many folks, but I think it's time to share it with you."

David kept his back to her.

"This is about my Thomas. We hadn't been long married. Thomas had a job on the railroad. Nothing fancy, but it was steady. We weren't rich folks; we didn't even have a car. But we'd managed to save enough for a down payment on this house, because it was old and a bit rundown, so it wasn't very expensive. Thomas said we could fix it up. And it was big enough for kids, which was important, because we wanted a large family."

There was a long pause.

"I wanted shutters on the house," Granny said softly. "All the fancy houses had them. They were just decoration, not real shutters for keeping anything out, but that was the fashion. When our babies came, I wanted them to feel proud of the house they were growing up in, so I kept saying to Thomas, 'Can't you put up some shutters?'

"We couldn't afford the kind you buy, but Thomas was always good with his hands, so he made some. Really nice ones. On each one he had cut out the shape of a flying bird, because he knew how much I loved watching the swallows in the backyard in summer. And he painted them a lovely sunshine yellow. I couldn't wait to see them up. I kept saying, 'Thomas, when are we going to get the shutters up?' He was working on the railroad all during the week and half the day on Saturday, so it was going to have to be a Sunday.

"One Sunday . . . at breakfast, I was saying, '*Please* put them up today. They've been sitting in the basement for two weeks now.' Often on Sundays Thomas would sit around all morning doing nothing except reading the

154

newspaper. Other folks would be going to church or getting out on a picnic, but all Thomas wanted to do was sit around. It was his only day off, he said, but I felt like he was wasting the day, so I kept nagging. Finally he said yes and went to do it. He put the shutters on the three downstairs windows while I made Sunday dinner. Then he got the ladder out to put the shutters up on that little window in your room. And . . ."

She stopped. David turned onto his back so he could look at her. Granny was gazing down at the bedspread, as if something interesting had appeared there.

"The shutter was too heavy for carrying up the ladder," she said at last. "Thomas got up there but . . . the ladder overbalanced. He dropped the shutter. I can remember hearing this splintery crash as it broke on the step. Then the ladder fell. And so did Thomas."

She looked over. "The way he fell, he hit his head on the step when he came down. He didn't die right away. In fact, it took him six weeks to do his dying, but he never woke up. From the moment when I told him to stop reading the papers and get out and hang those shutters, we never had another word together."

David lay very quietly.

"What I remember most is how horrible I felt about it. How guilty because I'd wanted something so silly. It was my fault Thomas was on that ladder that morning. If I hadn't been so vain about wanting a house just like other folks', maybe he'd still be alive. What I remember the very most, however, was this empty sort of feeling, as if a vacuum cleaner had come along and sucked out every-thing inside me.

"Sucked out my whole life. My whole world. Because in that instant everything changed. The person I loved most was gone. All the children we hadn't yet had were gone. Our future was gone. Our dreams. Everything. And nothing would ever be the same again."

"What did you do?" David asked.

Granny raised her shoulders slightly as if she were going to shrug, but she didn't. "Carried on," she said. "Things *weren't* ever the same again. They couldn't be. I had to learn to do all the things around the house that Thomas had done before. I had to earn money so I could pay the mortgage. I was so lonely. I didn't have Thomas, and without him I wasn't going to have children, either. I thought, 'I didn't choose this. It isn't fair.' But after time went by and I got more used to things, I thought, 'I didn't choose this, but it's the only life I've got.' So I reckoned I might as well do the best with it I could. I decided if I couldn't have my own family, I'd make a home for chil-dren who couldn't have their own families either. So that's what I did. Even now when I'm older and can't manage families of children anymore, I can still take one."

David let out a long, slow breath. "It-it *was* my fault King Arthur died," he said softly. "Because I broke up his nest. When he was just an egg. I-I never told anyone, not even Mab, but truth is, I-I didn't just find the egg. Why couldn't I have just left it alone? I wish that so much now."

156

Granny put a hand on his shoulder. "We all make mistakes. We all got things we regret doing."

Granny's image blurred as David's eyes filled with tears.

She said, "I know it's too soon right now, but what I've been thinking is that maybe we should get you a puppy. Mrs. Forman's daughter raises Jack Russells and Mrs. Forman was just telling me today how she's got a brand-new litter of puppies. She was telling me because she knows how much you like animals and thought you might like to come see them. That got me thinking that maybe, when they're old enough, you could have one. A Jack Russell's a good kind of dog for a boy to have. They love to learn tricks."

A special sort of sadness flooded David just then. If someone had asked him last week or even yesterday if he'd want a puppy of his own, David would have been jubilant. He'd always dreamed of having his own dog, especially one you could teach tricks to. Now, however, it only sounded awful. He didn't want some dog. He wanted King Arthur.

So he shook his head. "No."

"No, not right now. It's too soon. But these puppies have just been born, so they won't be ready to leave their mama for about eight weeks anyhow."

"I-I don't want a dog. What if it died too?"

Granny looked at him. "I wish I could tell you that after this, nothing bad is ever going to happen to you again, but the truth is, we just have to take our chances. No choice about that. Only choice we've got is what we do with ourselves when something happens, bad or good."

"K-King Arthur's dead. There's no choice in that."

"You're right, no choice about it happening. But you can choose what you do next."

"What's that mean?"

"If you're in a fight and you get knocked down, the other person doesn't automatically win, does he? Long as you keep getting back up, he hasn't beat you. It's only over when you keep laying there. So when something bad knocks you down, the first thing you do is get back up. This doesn't mean you don't hurt. And you don't have to pretend you don't. But if you get up, you haven't lost.

"The second choice is to decide to count good stuff. Think of King Arthur and start counting things like how you and Mab would never have been friends without him. Count how much fun you had hatching him out. And how you learned all sorts of things about owls. Count how you got a Saturday job because of him. Count how handsome he was and how he did such funny things."

"Th-that is so stupid. It's for little kids."

"No, not so. By counting the good stuff, you choose to make King Arthur matter. You choose to show the world you've turned out better because you knew him. Otherwise he's nothing but a dead owl."

TWENTY-FIVE

That evening the telephone rang. David was afraid it might be Mab and he didn't want to answer it, because he didn't know what to say. When Granny answered it and said it was for him, David gritted his teeth.

It wasn't Mab. It was Lily.

"Hey," she said, "remember me?" There was a joky tone to her voice. "You probably thought I dropped off the face of the earth, hey? Well, guess what? I'm back at the children's home."

David's head was too full of King Arthur for him to know what to say.

"Me and Mack broke up."

Silence.

"You're quiet. Even for you."

"M-my owl died. This morning." And so he told her. Even though Lily would probably laugh and call him stupid, David couldn't pretend everything was okay. So he explained how he and Mab had hatched the egg and raised King Arthur and now he'd died.

"Wow," Lily said when he'd finished. "Wow. I don't think I ever heard you say so many sentences together at once. You can be downright chatty, David. Cool. And cool about that owl."

"N-not cool. He *died*."

"Yeah, but cool you had him. You should have showed him to me when I was there," she said. "I would have liked to see that."

"He *died*."

"Yeah, that's tough." And then she paused. "Yeah. I'm sorry about that, David."

A little silence crept in, which was pretty unusual with Lily. She didn't do silences well.

"Things have been sort of tough with me too," she said, and her voice was softer. "You know, about going to see Mom? Well . . . I don't think, like, that lady was our mom. I mean, if she was . . . she didn't recognize me. She told me to go away."

A pause.

"Then me and Mack broke up. Which was just as well, I guess. I don't know. The police turned up. I think this lady called them. Then old Pruneface Mellor was there. And now I'm back here."

"P-probably it wasn't our mom."

Lily didn't say anything.

"M-maybe next time I can go with you. Maybe next time we'll find her."

160

"Yeah. Maybe next time."

"But I-I'm sorry it didn't happen this time," David said.

"Yeah." And then there was a small silence. "I'm sorry too, David. I'm sorry about your owl."

David had to go back to school the next day, even though throwing himself in front of a stampeding herd of water buffalo sounded like more fun. He couldn't imagine what he was going to say to Mab.

Granny must have figured this one out, because when David came down to breakfast, she said, "I phoned Mrs. Stopes yesterday and told her about King Arthur."

Well, at least that was something, David thought. He didn't have to surprise Mab with something nasty and then have her hate him. She could get on with hating him straightaway.

And this is what she seemed to do, because all morning Mab stayed well away. She didn't talk to him. She didn't look at him. Probably she didn't even want to be in the same room with him. David didn't blame her any.

In social studies they had to choose partners to go outside and count cars and trucks for their pollution graphs. The other girls paired up quickly. No one chose Mab.

Why did he never pick Mab? Because he was afraid of Rodney teasing about girlfriends or about their being freaks together? How stupid could you get? David felt ashamed, guilty, and sad all together.

Would you like to be my partner? He said the words in his head. He practiced them.

He didn't risk it. She'd say no now because she hated him. So, when Dennis came over, David just accepted that he was a coward, along with everything else, and went out with him.

At lunch break David stood against the wall behind the basketball court. He often passed the time there because it was always warm, even when it wasn't sunny, and he liked the rough feel of the bricks against his back. Better still, no teachers hassled him about joining in something, because they assumed he was watching the basketball game. Which sometimes he did do, but today he just stood.

He looked around the playground for Mab.

She was over by the side door, a jump rope in her hands. Rodney was there too. When Mab was jumping, he'd reach out every once in a while and stop the rope with a stick.

Actually there were a bunch of kids standing around over there, and David knew they were egging Rodney on. They weren't saying, "Do it! Do it!" because that was too obvious and the teachers would come. Instead they just stood around smiling, so that Rodney knew he was being cool.

That group picked on lots of kids that way. They'd done it to David and they'd done it to Dennis. Sometimes they did it to this girl in the other class named Tansy. Mostly they did it to Mab, because she always gave them a reaction and that's what they wanted.

Rodney was getting really elaborate about the way he approached Mab with his stick. He was using Irish jig steps to show off. Rodney had gotten his picture in the newspaper for winning a cup at a dance contest, so Mrs. Hallowell had let him dance the jig in front of the whole class. Now he Irish jigged on the playground. Step-step-step-step-turn. Poke the stick in Mab's jump rope. Making a dance out of it, like that's all it was to ruin someone's day.

Nobody tried to stop him. In fact, the others were enjoying themselves. It was okay to laugh because Mab was a freak.

David started to walk across the playground.

"Are you mad, Mad?" Rodney was saying, as he two-stepped up to the rope and tangled it. Clearly he thought this was hilarious to say, because he threw his head back, hooting like a howler monkey. "Are you mad, Mad?" He two-stepped away.

"S-s-stop it," David said.

"Rrrrrrowwww!" Rodney roared. The kid seemed to have a whole zoo in his vocal cords. "It's loverboy, come to the rescue!"

"S-stop it! Go pick on someone your own size."

"S-s-s-s-stop i-i-i-it!" Rodney mimicked. The kids standing around thought this was a stupendous joke. Several of them did it too under their breath. They sounded like a bunch of lisping snakes.

"D-does that sound funny to you?" David asked. "Want me to do it again? S-s-stop it." He exaggerated the *s* sound on purpose. "S-s-s-s-s-stop it."

Rodney looked at him. "You are such a freak, retardo."

"E-everyone's laughing, so I must be funny. Want me to do it again?" David asked. "S-s-s-s-s-stop it."

Rodney stared at David like he'd gone crazy.

"Want me to s-say it again?" David asked. "I mean, it is *so* f-funny. Wow! I'm a real comedian, huh? Ha, ha, ha. D-don't you think, everybody?"

"Man, you are such a freak it's not real," Rodney said at last.

"Yeah. S-so go away then," David said, and flung an arm out at him, "because I might freak out on you."

Rodney let the stick fall to the ground, but he didn't move.

"G-go on. All of you." David flung his arms widely out at the crowd of kids. "Because I'm d-dangerous too."

"Oh geez, the retard's finally lost it," Rodney said in a disgusted voice. But he did turn. "Come on, you guys. Let's quit wasting our time."

They all walked off together.

Silence followed.

Mab had her head down. She'd been trying hard not to show she was crying, but she was. Her eyes were watery and there was this little drip of snot.

David had hoped she'd say something about how brave he'd just been. He *had* been brave. Rodney was probably off plotting his revenge this very minute. David wished at least she'd say thank you.

But she didn't. She just stood there, head down, pretending not to cry.

"I-I'm sorry," David said very softly.

The silence stayed, drawing out long and uncomfortable.

"L-look, Mab, I'm really, really, *really* sorry about King Arthur. I-I'm so really, truly sorry I took him."

"You should be," Mab replied, her voice low. She wiped her eyes and didn't try to hide her tears any longer.

"P-probably it's my fault he died."

"Yes, probably it is."

"I-I am sorry. Honest. I mean that. I-I should have listened to your dad. I so, *so* wish I had let Dr. Pellam take him. I-I so wish I could make it Saturday again. I'd give anything in the world for that."

A long moment passed before Mab finally spoke.

"I cried so much last night," she finally said. "When my mom told me, I just couldn't believe it was true."

"I-I couldn't believe it when I saw," David replied. "I still hardly can. I still feel like if we went to the stall in the b-barn, he'd be there."

Mab nodded.

"It's the worst thing that's ever happened to me," Mab said.

"Y-yeah."

David shoved his hands in his pockets.

Finally Mab looked over. "Is it the worst thing that's ever happened to you?"

David let out a long breath. "I-I used to keep this list in my head. The Very Worst Things list. I thought I knew everything on it. W-worst was having nothing at all. No mom or dad. Not belonging anywhere or to anyone. Now

I think that's wrong. The very worst thing is having something and then losing it. B-because then you know how good the thing was that you lost."

"If that's true," Mab said quietly, "you wouldn't ever want to have *anything* good happen, because you might lose it."

"I dunno," David replied. "I-I was thinking about it last night. A lot."

Mab didn't say anything.

"I-I mean, I guess what makes a Very Worst Thing is that it was a Very Best Thing first. I think maybe you can't have one without the other."

"Maybe so," Mab said.

A long pause came.

"My dad said King Arthur probably wouldn't have lived anyhow," she murmured. "He says you can't take things out of the wild. They always die because it isn't where they belong. Even when you take good care of them."

"G-Granny says maybe I can get a dog," David replied. "Yesterday I-I said no, but . . . maybe later I'll say yes. It wouldn't be the same as K-King Arthur. . . . But I've always wanted a dog. And Granny says it's the kind that learns tricks."

Mab nodded.

"M-maybe you could help me teach it tricks," David suggested. "I-I mean, if you wanted. Because I wouldn't know where to start. But maybe you've got a book on it. Or something."

Mab nodded.

They just stood. David watched the other kids, the ones who had been picking on Mab, on the far side of the playground. Rodney was taking a turn at Chinese jump rope. It wasn't the kind of thing you'd think he'd do, but he was good at it.

"E-everyone really calls you Mad, don't they?" David asked. It was a stupid question a million miles away from what they'd been talking about, but it just came to him. "Truth is, I'm the only one who calls you Mab, huh?"

She didn't answer.

"Th-they make fun of me, you know. They think I can't say your name right, that it's my stutter."

"It really is Mab," she said in a low voice.

"But you don't get Mab from Madeleine."

"No, maybe not, but it's still Mab. For me. Inside me. Just like you are King Arthur inside. So I let you call me that, because you're my friend."

David smiled slightly.

The other kids on the playground ran about, screaming and yelling cheerfully. Mab and David remained quietly against the wall.

"W-want to be friends again?" David asked.

She didn't answer right away, but at last she gave a little half shrug, as if a fly had landed on her shoulder. "I guess."

"Y-you don't have to," he said because she had sounded so uncertain. "I-I'd understand."

"When I was talking to my dad last night, he said it wasn't fair to blame everything on you. Really, it was sort of my fault too. I didn't want to give King Arthur to Dr.

Pellam either, so when you took King Arthur, I didn't tell on you. . . ." She lifted her eyes and looked past him, up into the sky. "If you want to know the truth, I wished *I* could have run away with King Arthur too. What made me *mad* at you—I mean, King Arthur dying just made me really sad—but what made me *mad* was that you ran away without me. You never talked to me about it. You never even stopped to think I might be on your side."

"I-I didn't mean that," David said. "M-my sister used to do that to me all the time, so I know what it feels like. I'm sorry."

"I don't think friends should do that. Friends belong together."

David nodded.

She looked over. Looked him up and down very thoroughly and finally gave a tired little smile with her lips pressed tightly together. Then she held out her hand flat so that David could give her five. David turned enough to do it properly, so that it made a resounding smack.

They both leaned back against the wall again. It was almost time for the bell to ring.

"So . . ." Mab said, "want to come over after school?"

"And do what? W-we haven't got King Arthur to take care of."

"We could do other stuff. If you wanted to hatch something, we could see if the ducks are laying. They're loads easier to raise."

"They d-don't eat dead mice, do they?"

Mab grinned. "No. Just duck pellets."

David looked off across the playground.

"What I-I was thinking . . ." he said slowly. "Maybe we could read *Lord of the Rings*. I'm probably going to be a g-grandpa before I can read it myself."

She smiled, her eyes going crinkly in the corners. "Yeah, that would be good."

"Okay. But I-I'll need to tell Granny. I'll come out later. First I'll go home."